MURDER ON HOLDIDAY ISLAND

A CYPRUS COVE COZY MYSTERY

Liz Turner

Copyright © 2021 by Liz Turner.

All rights reserved. No part of this publication may be reproduced, distributed or transmitted in any form or by any means, including photocopying, recording, or other electronic or mechanical methods, without the prior written permission of the publisher, except in the case of brief quotations embodied in critical reviews and certain other noncommercial uses permitted by copyright law.

Publisher's Note: This is a work of fiction. Names, characters, places and incidents are a product of the author's imagination. Locales and public names are sometimes used for atmospheric purposes. Any resemblance to actual people, living or dead, or to businesses, companies, events, institutions, or locales is completely coincidental.

Contents

Chapter 1 Surprise Visitors 5

Chapter 2 Interfering Friends 17

Chapter 3 Disastrous Dining 26

Chapter 4 Intolerable Chef vs Insufferable Diner 34

Chapter 5 The Italian Villagers..50

Chapter 6 Amateur Sleuth 62

Chapter 7 Burn the Evidence 71

Chapter 8 Facing the Past..84

Chapter 9 Moonlit Confessions 90

Chapter 10 A Final Kitchen Run 102

Chaper 11 A Second Chance 109

Chapter 1
Surprise Visitors

"Just a touch of cadmium yellow over here," Isabel said while pointing at the canvas with the end of her paintbrush.

"I thought so too," Rosemary agreed, dabbing her brush into a tiny splotch of untainted cadmium amongst a mess of rich color playing across her palette.

Isabel Austin stood back and admired her most diligent student's oil painting. A cobalt sea housed a range of cheerful bathers splashing in the waves and darting back to picnic baskets and colorful towels on the shore.

"It looks spectacular and radiates happiness," Isabel complimented her. "You've been working on this for months," Isabel smiled with approval, "and now that it's complete, it makes me long for a morning on the beach instead of one in the studio."

"I think her dirty palette is more exciting than that boring beach scene," a grouchy woman in the corner mumbled under her breath. She wore leopard print from head to toe and insisted on wearing six-inch heels despite being in her seventies.

"At least I don't keep painting nudes, Deborah," Rosemary fired scornfully back at the obnoxious woman.

"Now, now," Isabel interrupted the pair from the retirement village, "each student in this class has their own unique taste. And we don't need to hurl paint at each other's paintings to show we disagree with what someone else is doing." She eyed Debbie's painting of a nude woman positioned on a Persian carpet, eating grapes, and she shuddered. "But we can all benefit from a little positive criticism."

"Precisely," Debbie snorted and flicked a red dyed and permed curl over her shoulder.

"What I was going to say to you, Isabel," Rosemary continued sweetly, "was that I think you should take a holiday. You've been slogging away in this studio, teaching class after class, and working on your own paintings at all hours of the night."

"Yes, teacher Isabel," a second student piped up, "you should book yourself away for a weekend. Go and visit one of the neighboring islands and explore the area more!"

"Thanks Peter, but I just don't have the time," Isabel shrugged and stooped to swoop up a grey ball of fluff into her arms.

The grey fluff meowed and purred with delight. A white socked paw darted out and playfully swiped at her hand.

"You could take that handsome detective of yours along with you," Debbie uttered in a sultry voice.

Isabel snorted with embarrassment and her face reddened instantly.

"Our relationship is not on that level!" Isabel replied defensively. "And even if it was, it's not professional to share that level of information with my students."

"If you don't move a little faster," Debbie warned her with a flutter of her fake eyelashes and a red-lipped grin, "I might snatch him up myself."

"Oh please, Debs, you've tried and failed on many occasions," another elderly woman said with a cackle. "The detective is besotted with our young teacher and no other woman, no matter how desperate her offer, stands a chance with him."

Debbie muttered to herself in a grumbling tone as she reached for the crimson tube of paint. She dabbed colors on viciously, her canvas shaking dangerously on the unsteady easel.

Isabel laughed and shook her head. "I enjoy the peace of my studio. Although, I think I'd enjoy it a lot more if my students fought less, but we can't have everything."

There was a rippled of laughter through the studio space, followed by the contemplative silence of artists at work. Brushes could be heard swishing through glasses of turpentine, then poking into blobs of color, and finally swabbing against stretched canvases. The smells and sounds were calming to Isabel.

She set down her purring cat, who stretched and found her way to a patch of sunlight near the front door. Isabel walked to the coffee station, her hand stroking along the sleek, black back of a second cat.

"Hello, Harry," she greeted him with a kiss on the nose, which he did not entirely hate, though he squinted his green eyes at her.

Isabel filled up the coffee machine and soon the scent of roasted coffee beans wafted through the entire studio.

Isabel pulled out the milk and had to fight off her third, and fattest, cat, Tinkles. He meowed ferociously at the milk bottle and seemed determined to claw his way up her leg.

A soft-hearted Isabel relented and poured some milk into a saucer, which was immediately beset upon by three thirsty cats.

Isabel smiled at the group of chattering students that oozed excitement as they experimented with the thrills and pitfalls of oil paint. Around them, her studio was a quiet, free space that encouraged anyone to walk through the entrance and find the inspiration to create. Pride flowed through every vein as she contemplated all she had accomplished in her short time in Cyprus Cove.

Isabel's thoughts strayed to her disapproving parents, who had forbidden her from pursuing a career as a worthless artist. She smiled to herself and wondered what they would say if they could see her newly found confidence as a working woman, surviving in an unfamiliar town on her own. Would they admit defeat when they were forced to acknowledge her success as an artist? Would they admire her for the love she had permitted herself to find since she had left their oppressive care?

The door burst open, interrupting Isabel's pensive state. Two dogs and a cat hurtled in with excited yaps and howls, an enormous Great Dane making his way straight for the milk saucer and sending her three cats scuttling in fright. Milly, the grey cat, tried to claw her way up a flow of leopard print fabric, causing Debbie to leap forward in fright and slap her voluptuous figure into her wet painting.

The second dog, a filthy, dreadlocked poodle mix, darted through Peter's legs, resulting in him losing his balance and knocking his easel over. It toppled onto Pearl's which fell forward with a wet thwack onto the wooden floorboards. It instantly filled the room with gasps and shrieks as one canvas went down after another. Isabel glanced around in horror, spotting her all-black cat with a streak of cobalt blue in his fur as he bolted away.

"No!" she groaned with growing dread, her eyes finding the beautiful seascape painting lying face up on the floor and obscured by a series of paw prints, which had also dotted a maze of color all over her wooden floorboards.

"Well," a shrill voice boomed, "this is not much of a studio, is it. A bit of a mess, but I expected little else from our youngest."

Isabel's face paled as a pair of plump buttocks reversed through her front entrance and turned around, revealing a familiar red-faced woman.

"Mother!" Isabel bleated in horror, like a terrified sheep watching a vicious wolf break into her pen.

"Darling!" her mother crooned at her over the chaotic din of barking dogs and shrieking cats. The large woman swanned elegantly across the splotches of oil paint and shredded pieces of canvases, to enforce an unwelcome hug on her shocked daughter.

"Wh... wh..." Isabel took a breath and tried again. "What are you doing here?"

"What do you mean, what am I doing here? Don't I have a right to visit my youngest, darling daughter after she flees her home and refuses to talk to us?"

"I didn't -" Isabel attempted, but her attention was drawn to her rake-like father, who had just heaved an enormous trunk through the front door of her studio. "What's with the luggage?" Isabel demanded, her voice shrill in her own ears.

"You can't expect us to wear the same clothes for the next three weeks," her mother chortled, her pair of chins wagging with mirth.

"Three weeks," Isabel squeaked, her chest closing in and tiny sparkling dots forming in front of her eyes.

She felt a warm, gentle hand take her by the arm and support her.

"Hi, I'm Rosemary, Isabel's first student. Your daughter is just an absolute delight, and we all love having her here as our art teacher."

A chorus of warm agreement sounded from her students scattered around the room. Many had been splattered with paint or knocked over by a leaping dog, but mostly they were unharmed.

"There's no such thing as an *art teacher*," her mother laughed. "It's just an absurd notion people create to provide a career title for people who don't have proper jobs."

"Colleen, love, be kind," Isabel's father delicately leapt to her defense. "You promised we'd give Izzie's new life a fair chance."

Colleen clicked her tongue at her husband and both dogs responded by hurrying to her side, their tails rotating with excitement.

"Parentals," Isabel hissed between gritted teeth, "I don't mean to be disrespectful, but why are you here?"

"We missed you," her father said softly, his big brown eyes brimming with sincerity.

Isabel smiled at him, her own matching eyes warming at his kindness. She took after him in appearance, though her blonde hair hung down her back and she had her mother's curls.

"You can't stay here," Isabel stated weakly, though inside she knew she had already lost the battle.

"Are you going to force your parents to sleep on the street?" Colleen demanded.

Isabel noticed that her students, who had silently been picking up the destroyed fragments of their paintings and swiping up the muddy oil paint from the floorboards, now quickly hurried out the front door to the relative safety of the streets.

Rosemary, her dear friend, offered an apologetic wave and blew a kiss as she hobbled quickly out the door.

Isabel sighed and recalled her mind to her mother's accusation. "Of course not, but do you even realize that your unannounced arrival destroyed my entire art class this afternoon? People pay good money to be here -"

"That's quite enough complaining," Colleen stated firmly. "You should be happy to see us."

Though Isabel's mother was a pretty looking woman with gentle brown curls that framed her chubby cheeks, and delightful green eyes that smiled at everyone, she was impossible to defy.

"Don't talk to your mother like that," her father added with a stern nod of his head.

"Thank you, Robert. I was wondering when you were going to step in and defend me," she said a little tartly.

Isabel fought not to roll her eyes and scream with frustration. Her worst nightmare had barged belligerently through the door of her studio and moved in for three weeks. Her mind snatched at loose threads to try to make out how they had located her. Isabel had only provided a vague location as 'at the sea', so unless they had visited every single seaside town to track her down like a runaway dog, then she did not know how they had found her.

"I just have one question," Isabel asked in her most patient voice, though her heart was threatening to rip out her chest. "How did you find me?"

Colleen snorted, not unlike a pig, and folded a pair of dimpled hands in front of her. "Your friend invited us, of course."

Isabel repeated the words breathlessly. Her immediate and callous thoughts were that none of her real friends would betray her like that.

"Which friend?" Isabel asked specifically, her eyes watching her mother closely.

"Oh," her mother waved a hand and clicked her tongue again, "enough of the technicalities. Where will your father and I be sleeping?"

Isabel felt every muscle in her body tense up and her bones grew so rigid she knew they would snap if she took a single step. The blood pulsed through her veins, and her hands clenched into fists as she glowered at her mother, who was obliviously fussing over her mutts.

"Uh... am I interrupting something?" an uncertain voice sounded at the front door.

Isabel realized she had heard, but not acknowledged, the squeak of her front door. Someone had walked into the studio space and was staring at her. She forced her gaze from her mother and found friendly grey eyes questioning her.

"Ricardo," Isabel stammered, her tongue thick and uncooperative.

His lips twitched into an awkward smile and his focus flickered to her mother and father. "Are you going to introduce us?" he asked in an amiable tone.

Isabel jerked out of her blazing fury. "Of course," she choked the words out. "Ricardo, this is my mother, Colleen, and my father, Robert. They've arrived for a... surprise visit. Apparently one of my 'friends' invited them."

Isabel could not help the strangled squeak of the voice that escaped her tight throat. She had made the last sentence sound like an accusation, and Ricardo responded instantly with a 'not guilty' expression.

Isabel noticed her mother's eyebrow spike with curiosity as she studied the handsome man standing in her daughter's studio and holding a bouquet of wildflowers he had just picked.

"And Mother, Father, this is," Isabel coughed slightly, "detective Ricardo Finch."

"It's a pleasure to meet you," Robert said, breaking the spell of awkwardness that had settled on the room. He stepped forward and extended his hand in a gesture of gentlemanly friendliness.

"And how do you know our daughter?" Colleen inquired with a sly expression.

Isabel fired the smallest of head shakes at Ricardo before he answered.

"Well," he took a deep breath and laughed slightly, "we work on the occasional police case together."

Colleen overflowed with snorts and giggles, even swiping a tear away from her eye.

"You're a funny one," she joked.

Ricardo frowned slightly. He had not been joking.

"I'm quite serious, Mrs. Austin," he insisted. "Your daughter has an incredible mind and, more than that, an artistic eye that often helps us find clues we would never have uncovered without her help. She's been a real asset to the local police station."

Colleen had not seemed to absorb a single word. Her face took on a blank expression, and she pursed her lips, as though deliberately refusing to accept the wild notion that her dense daughter possessed an ounce of intelligence. There was no way Isabel, who could not successfully boil an egg, or do a load of white washing without it turning pink, could possess undiscovered skills anyone else could find valuable.

"Alright then," Colleen concluded with apparent dismissal. "Tell me, Ricardo, are those flowers for her?"

Isabel felt her stomach twist painfully into a tense knot of internal destruction. She fired a silent accusation at the universe, demanding to know what she had done to deserve the meteor-like collision that was imminently about to destroy everything she had built up.

"No," Ricardo laughed convincingly, his grey eyes dancing with light. "I had heard that you would visit, and I thought some of our colorful countryside would be a fitting way to welcome you to Cyprus Cove."

Colleen giggled profusely, her cheeks reddening as she bashfully snatched the flowers from Ricardo and buried her face in the colorful scents.

"How kind of you," she gushed. "Thank you, these are just lovely. Oh, I just knew Isabel would find wonderful friends here to look after her."

"For the most part, she looks after us," Ricardo forced another compliment in.

To his surprise, Colleen laughed even louder. "Isabel?" she snorted, her voice dripping with condescension. "She can't even scramble eggs, let alone look after anyone. I've always done everything for her."

Isabel picked up Milly, who had a smear of cerise pink on her head, and drew her close.

Ricardo chuckled politely. "Don't worry, I can assist with the cooking while you are here so that you won't have to suffer through Isabel's dangerous cooking."

Colleen looked impressed. "You'll make a fine catch for a fine lady, detective."

Isabel smiled at Ricardo from behind Milly's head. Her little safe world had crumbled around her within seconds, as the oppressive shadows from her past had crept in unwelcomed. But with Ricardo standing a few feet away and warmly joking with her parents, who clearly instantly adored him, she knew she could survive, as long as she had him by her side.

"Come on," Isabel sighed and managed a weary smile. "Let me show you to your room."

Chapter 2
Interfering Friends

Isabel, seated on the sofa, had surrounded herself with a stash of protective cats. A suitcase, which exploded with items of clothing that sought to escape the stuffed space, stood at her feet.

"So, let me see if I have this straight. You want to stay at my place because your parents are visiting?"

"Don't give me that look, Rachel," Isabel whined. "You have no idea how bad they are!"

Rachel leapt off her chair and closed her office door. She studied Isabel with serious eyes. "But they're your parents, Iz!"

"Look, I know you're some hardcore detective who's made a niche for yourself in the male dominated police world, and so you're not afraid of anything, but my mother terrifies me," Isabel explained, gripping Milly closer.

"I thought everyone loved surprise visits from their parents," Rachel muttered.

"Wait," Isabel focused sharply on her detective friend while relinquishing her hold on the cat, "don't tell me you're the 'friend' who invited them for here in the first place!"

Rachel maintained her poker face for a few solid minutes before she cracked into a guilty grin.

"I'm so sorry!" she blurted out loudly. "I thought I was doing a good thing!"

"How could you do this to me! I literally packed my bags, and my precious cat babies, and ran away from them! How would bringing them back help me in any way?"

"You need to face your fears," Rachel informed her sternly.

"Why?" Isabel demanded loudly, causing her cats to scatter to safe hiding places in the maze of filing cabinets and boxes of evidence.

"Because if you and Ricardo are romantically serious about each other, which I think you are, then you need to make peace with your past before you can successfully confront your future."

"Did you read that off a candy wrapper?" Isabel accused her angrily. "Because stuff like that doesn't work in the real world!"

Rachel huffed and slammed her hands onto her hips. "I thought I was helping."

"Oh, you're going to help, alright," Isabel insisted. "By letting me and my fur children sleep on your couch for the next three weeks."

"I will not do that," Rachel replied stubbornly.

Isabel felt hot tears spring to her eyes. "Please," she begged, out of sheer desperation.

"No. And the reason is that I planned something else for your parents and you."

Isabel's eyes remained fixed on Rachel while her hand reached blindly for her forearm so that she could pinch herself to try to wake from the nightmare her own friend had brought on.

"I booked you away for the weekend," Rachel added with a callous grin. "I thought it would be… you know… kind of cool."

Isabel collapsed onto the grim sofa Rachel's office sported, sending the newly settled Tinkles flying in fright.

"Look, you might not always have your parents around," Rachel said seriously.

Isabel caught the tragic note that lilted her voice. "What are you not telling me?"

Rachel scooted off the edge of her desk and stalked to her window, where she stared out with an air of drama. Harry hopped off a box of police case files and slid his silky body around her ankles.

"What happened to your parents?" Isabel asked gently.

"They died when I was a teenager," she explained in a husky voice. "Before that, I wanted nothing to do with them because I thought they were old and boring. After the accident, all I wanted was to go back and savor every minute I'd ever had with them, but once you reach that point it's already too late."

"I'm sorry," Isabel said weakly, her hand reaching for Rachel's broad shoulder. "I did not know you'd been through so much."

"Most people don't know. I refuse to let people feel sorry for me," she said gruffly. "But I don't want you to settle down here, marry Ricardo, and never see your parents again, because before you know it, you may not have the option to ever see them again."

Isabel stared out at the jagged surface of the tumultuous sea, noting the white peaks whipped out by the wind. The weather reflected her mood.

"Thank you," Isabel managed, her throat thick.

"For?"

"For caring enough about me to step in and try to prevent me from enduring the same pain you did."

Isabel watched her tough friend blush slightly. "You've saved my back plenty of times. Not to mention all the cases you've helped us solve. This is the least I can do."

Her door vibrated with incessant pounding, causing Isabel to jolt in fright. This led to three anxious cats leaping into her arms from all directions.

"They've found me," Isabel hissed to herself, her eyes wide with terror.

Ricardo did not wait for a reply. He burst in and glowered at Rachel.

"You booked *me* off this weekend using *your* leave days! Is that even allowed?" he questioned her.

"Jeez, I thought you'd be a little more appreciative," Rachel snapped. "It's free leave."

She poured herself another mug of strong black coffee and slurped at it noisily, her eyes twinkling with mischief.

"I don't get it," Ricardo blasted again. "Why are you being so nice? It's totally not like you at all."

"Rachel was the friend who surprise-asked my parents to visit," Isabel explained. "Her intentions were good, and I think she might be right. I've cut my parents out for too long, and if you're going to be part of my life, it's only fair you get to know them."

"Exactly," Rachel smirked at Ricardo. "Besides, partner, how are you going to ask Isabel's father for her hand in marriage if the two of you never have a conversation?"

Ricardo paled instantly and then his tanned face flooded red at the mention of marriage.

"It is your intention to marry her, right?" Rachel continued, enjoying the merciless torture she was inflicting on her partner. "Because I'm sure Isabel's parents are bound to ask."

"Alright, enough," Isabel interrupted the cat fight that was about to break out. "What's your big plan for us, Rachel? You mentioned an island?"

"Yes, San Nikos," Rachel expanded with a cheerful smile. "Have you ever been there before?"

Isabel shook her head. She had been nowhere except her hometown and college before she moved to Cyprus Cove.

"Then you're in for a real treat. You'll get to enjoy gorgeous beaches, delicious food, and a fun-filled stress-free weekend."

"How could you afford San Nikos?" Ricardo demanded.

Despite trusting Rachel with his life every day on the job, Ricardo was still cautious with Rachel's friendship. She was a smart woman and had a way of getting people to do what she needed them to do without them realizing it. Ricardo had been outwitted one too many times.

"I have a friend there who owes me a favor," Rachel replied curtly.

"You don't have any other friends besides us," Ricardo informed her. "I need a name of said friend so that I know I can trust you. That's after I've run several background checks."

Rachel rolled her eyes and flicked her hair behind her ears.

"Kendra Waters, okay! I helped on a case a few years ago at her restaurant. She said she owed me one, so I called in a favor. She owns a seriously fancy restaurant and resort. So, I will also provide your dinner on the night of your arrival, all expenses included."

Isabel sank her head into her hands and shook it.

"What's wrong?" Ricardo sympathized.

"You do not know how much my mother can eat," Isabel wailed.

"It will be okay. This will be good for all of you."

"Wait, what do you mean *'all* of us'?" Ricardo repeated.

"Yeah, thus the weekend off. You're going too, lover boy."

Isabel smiled at him. "I'm sure I will survive a weekend with my parents if Ricardo is there."

"Yeah," he offered them a smug look, "your parents already love me."

"That's because they don't know you're dating their daughter," Rachel pointed out.

"I think they'll just love me more when I tell them," Ricardo replied.

Rachel gave Isabel a knowing smile.

"What was that look about?" Ricardo asked quickly, spotting the exchange between the women, which had silently spoken volumes.

"No time to explain," Rachel said with a clap of her hands. "I will babysit your flea sacks while you're away."

"You mean my cats," Isabel corrected her. "And I'm not so sure that's such a good idea. You're terrible with animals."

"Tinkles likes me," Rachel replied defensively.

"Tinkles," Isabel said, referring to the largest and scruffiest of the three cats, "likes anyone with food."

"I don't care *why* he likes me, as long as he does. Anyway," she waved a hand, "I will babysit for the weekend. Right, you two need to pack. Your island getaway is waiting."

Isabel had been more than impressed with their little chalet that opened out onto the beach. She smiled to herself, still unable to believe how she and Ricardo were on the tiny island that was bathed in magic and the breathtaking splendor of nature.

Isabel felt a hand slip into hers and squeeze it gently.

"It's still hard to imagine we're actually standing here on a Friday afternoon," Ricardo whispered, his voice barely audible over the crash of waves against the shore. "No police cases to worry about. Just you and me."

"Is that what you're wearing to dinner?" Colleen's voice slammed into them.

Isabel jerked her hand out of Ricardo's and leapt away from him.

"And my parents," Isabel mumbled, a surly expression creeping onto her usually endearing features.

"You look terrific," Colleen said with a snort and winking at Ricardo.

"As do you, Mrs. Austin," Ricardo returned the compliment. "See, they love me," he hissed into Isabel's ear as soon as Colleen's back was turned.

"Izzie, darling, won't you check on your father? Ricardo will escort me to the restaurant."

Isabel knew better than to protest. She knocked politely on her father's bedroom door and waited for a reply.

"Isabel, dear, you look bewitching in that dress," her father said with a warm smile. "It's almost as though you're trying to impress someone, and I highly doubt that someone is your mother or I. Anyway, I've missed you dearly, my precious girl."

"The best part is that it has pockets," Isabel responded daftly to the compliment.

Isabel felt her heart ache at his fatherly warmth. She always felt that her father was a different person when her mother was not around. It was as though he would see her with his own eyes, instead of through his wife's tainted ones.

Isabel nodded. There had been times when she had wanted to bundle everything back inside her powder blue Ford Escort, including her three prized cats, and accept the ease of the life she had endured where her parents had done everything for her.

"You look happy here," her father said, nudging her in the side with his elbow. "Are you?"

"I am," Isabel answered truthfully. "I've had some tough days, but I really feel like I'm discovering who I am, and who I want to be, without being told who I should be."

"By your mother and I, you mean," he said with a twinkle in his eye.

"Sorry," Isabel lowered her gaze, "I didn't mean to seem ungrateful for all the guidance you've offered over the years."

"I'm proud of you for sticking it out as long as you have. But," he turned serious blue eyes on her, "I don't want you to believe that you have to flee from those who love you just to discover who you think you are."

Isabel absorbed this quietly. She knew better than to argue with her father, for he never wasted a word. He said little, but when he was in the mood to offer advice, she knew it was best to listen.

"And the young man?" he prompted, with a second nudge to her ribs.

Isabel laughed nervously. "Perhaps we can discuss that over dinner."

Chapter 3
Disastrous Dining

"What do you mean you don't serve Lobster Thermidor," Colleen demanded. "This is a top-class restaurant, is it not?"

"Yes, ma'am," the waiter apologized profusely. He had a mess of brown hair on his head and was ruggedly handsome, though Mrs. Austin seemed to strip him of his manliness. "The problem is that Lobster Thermidor is not on our menu."

"Surely the chef is a qualified man and can simply cook one up for me?" Colleen demanded further.

"My dear," Robert interrupted gently, "why not order something different? You've never even had lobster before, so you don't know if you'll actually like it."

"Precisely why I want to order it!" she squealed. "We're not paying for any of this, so we may as well get the most out of it."

Though Isabel never drank, she was eyeing Ricardo's beer as though it was a tantalizing delicacy she had yet to experience.

"Perhaps you could choose one of our other seafood dishes," the waiter suggested with a trembling smile.

"Ugh," Colleen said, making a face, "I can hardly stomach seafood."

Isabel reached for Ricardo's beer and took a swig, her face pulling from the bitterness. Ricardo gently set a hand on her forearm and forced her to lower his glass.

Isabel's mother was too preoccupied with the waiter to even notice. She was paging furiously through the voluminous menu to find something that would meet her approval.

"Excuse me," Ricardo squinted at the waiter's gold nametag, "Ross. Why not bring a starter platter for us. That way Mrs. Austin can sample a few of the appetizers and then select her main course later."

Colleen clapped her hands together and beamed at Ricardo. "Genius!" she enthused. "Pure genius. Thank you for coming to my rescue, Ricardo. I wish my husband had been so sensitive to my needs."

Robert stroked his wife's hand with his own. "Sorry, my dear, it's just I noticed something while you were talking to the waiter."

"Mmm," she raised her eyebrows at him, as though she was surprised her husband was in the habit of observing anything. "And what might that have been?"

Robert swiped a finger between Isabel and the detective, his eyes narrowing on them.

"You two look awfully cosey sitting there next to each other," he pointed out, the corner of his mouth twitching up into a smile.

Isabel flushed hot, but Ricardo's mouth split into a wide smile that refused to hide his emotions.

"Don't do it," Isabel cautioned between gritted teeth.

"It's funny you mention that, Mr. Austin," Ricardo began confidently.

Isabel watched as her mother lowered her lemonade and frowned at Ricardo, her eyes squinting dangerously.

"Isabel and I began as friends. But as time passed by, we found something else growing between us. We've been dating for the last few months, and we wanted to use this weekend to tell you about us."

"Have you made her an offer of marriage?" Colleen demanded.

Ricardo was too stunned to talk. He stared at her, his lips opening and closing mutely.

"Not as yet," he stuttered.

"Then are you just using my daughter to fornicate with -"

"What!" Isabel exploded with disgust. "Gross, no!"

"It's not like that. We have a wholesome relationship," Ricardo explained tactfully.

"So, all this nicety has just been your way of winning yourself into our good books so that you can run away with our daughter, right under our noses?" Colleen demanded.

"No, ma'am," Ricardo squeaked, his usually deep voice deserting him. "We just thought you would want to know."

"Our daughter is a little too young to date," Robert added to support his wife, though his eyes looked away from Isabel.

"I'm twenty-five!" Isabel erupted, her hand reaching for Ricardo's beer again, which he smoothly whipped out of reach.

"No dear, I think you're twenty-four," her mother had the nerve to correct her.

"No, she can't be over twenty-two," her father gasped.

Isabel rolled her eyes. This had been the exact fight that had led her to pack her bags, throw her art trunk and her cats into her ancient car, and speed off to the other side of the country. Her parents' absolute refusal to acknowledge her as an adult capable of making her own decisions had not changed.

"Regardless of her age," Ricardo said, quelling the flames, "Isabel and I are an item."

"I see," Colleen replied primly, her face vacant of her former smiles. "And how are you to provide for her?"

"I have a good income as a detective."

Colleen exhaled slowly, her cheeks pink from the exertion.

"That's dangerous work, son," Robert observed. "How do we know you'll live long enough to keep our daughter safe?"

"That's what I love about your daughter," Ricardo explained with a smile. "She's not afraid of my work. Rather, she embraces it and even jumps headfirst into some of our cases -"

"You allow her in the path of danger?" Colleen accused. "How could you ever be a suitable partner for her?"

"What about your family? Do you have a big family?" Robert changed the subject.

"Rather small," Ricardo replied. "I'm an only child -"

"That simply won't do," Colleen said shaking her head back and forth. "Our Isabel is used to an enormous family that loves her. She will never survive if she only has you around."

"Yes, that's true. Isabel loves having all of us around."

Ross chose the perfect moment to deliver the enormous platter into the center of the table. He did so with a flourish and was expectant of a few 'oohs' and 'ahs', but the somber table tucked in with vicious intent, hardly noticing the golden crumbed mushrooms as they were dunked into sauce, or the steamed dumplings, or the delicate roast quails.

"Are you ready to order your mains?" Ross asked politely, his hand positioned behind his back, resting against a pristine white jacket with perfect buttons.

The steely silence provided his answer and Ross snuck away from the awkward table, returning with a bottle of 'wine on the house'. He poured everyone a glass and slunk away into a dark corner, lamenting the day he had become a waiter.

After watching her mother filch the last quail away from Ricardo with her fork, Isabel decided she needed to break the silence and put into action everything she had learned from her time in Cyprus Cove. She needed to stand up for herself and voice her feelings to her parents. It was her fault they walked all over her, since she always compromised and never divulged what was really in her heart.

"During this entire conversation," Isabel said with serious determination to get through the speech she had been working on in her head, "neither of you," her eyes flicked between her parents, "have ever asked what *I* wanted."

"I *know* what you want," her mother countered in a soothing voice. "I'm your mother. I've known what's best for you from day one."

"No," Isabel shook her head firmly. She heard her mother's fork rattle against the China plate as she dropped it. "You *think* you know what I want, but you've never actually asked me. That's why I took my cats –"

"Our cats -"

"*My* cats and moved so far away. I needed to discover who I was on my own. I needed to see what I could accomplish when I was standing on my own two feet. And it has blown me away by what I can do. I've started my own art studio -"

"With Delta's help," her mother chipped in.

"No," Isabel cut her off. "I pay the rent there. Those are my students and I make a living out of a career that you said would never pay me a cent. For the first time in years, I'm painting, and drawing and feeling creatively happy, not stifled by the oppressive cloud that hung over me when I lived with you."

Her father looked down at his plate while her mother turned tearful and scarlet. Colleen dabbed her napkin into the corner of her eye.

"I didn't know we were so terrible to live with. Here I thought we were providing the best possible life for you, and you just couldn't wait to get away from us!"

"Now, now, Colleen love, you did the best you could," Robert soothed, his hand rubbing his wife's enormous back.

"The point is, you did your best for me, but at some point, you have to let me go. I love Ricardo. He's good to me and he's really trying to attempt to be good to you. You need to let me grow up."

Colleen opened her mouth to retaliate, but Robert placed his hand on hers and gave it a little squeeze.

"It's hard," he said in a croaky voice and with eyes that glistened in light, "you're our little girl and we haven't wanted to let you leave because then we'd be alone."

"But in keeping me stuck there, you've pushed me away," Isabel voiced her genuine feelings. "Living with you all that time was suffocating. You made every decision for me, told me how to do any small job and then usually whipped it out of my hands and did it yourself."

"That's because we know what's best!" Colleen insisted. "You're too young to have an opinion."

"Darling, our Izzie is twenty-five now," Robert stated calmly and with finality. "She's right. We do have to let her live a little, otherwise she'll never grow."

Ross, who had quietly been clearing the table in between the heated conversation, pulled out his notepad to take down their mains.

"But I don't want to let her go," Colleen said, erupting into hot tears. "She's my baby and always will be!"

Ross shoved his notepad back into his apron and scampered away as quickly as his feet could carry him across the plush carpets. His black mop of hair bobbed as he walked, and his white-gloved hands fidgeted with his buttons.

"It doesn't mean I'll stop loving you," Isabel forced herself to say the words.

"It seems like you have," Colleen blubbered. "No letters, no phone calls, no post cards! We had to scour online newspapers, for months, before we spotted your name in an article about a forged painting and a murder. We got hold of your detective friend, Rachel, and she told us where you lived."

"I'm sorry, I was just worried that if I contacted you, you would pack up and come here, which you did. You don't trust me."

"We're learning to," Robert cut in before his wife could. He smiled warmly at his daughter. "Your mother will come around, Iz, but you need to give us time."

Isabel sighed, the relief tangible. She felt as though a weight had dropped from her heavy heart and she had made space for more in her life. Her own eyes blurred with tears and soon she was sobbing, almost as loudly as her mother was.

"Now," Colleen slapped her hands together, "all this crying and fighting has awakened my appetite. Where's that blasted waiter?"

Ross charged over from his place against the wall, where he had been talking to a gorgeous red head, the anxiety clear in his dark brown eyes.

"Ready to order?" he quavered.

"Yes, and it's about time you showed up," Colleen snapped.

Chapter 4
Intolerable Chef vs Insufferable Diner

"I'm just going to the ladies," Isabel said, excusing herself.

As she wound her way through the elegant tables, she noticed their waiter was chatting to the redhead again. The redhead laughed gently, and the light glinted on her manager badge. A booming holler from the kitchen sent Ross skittering along the floor to collect an order. It looked like their table's order.

Isabel could hear the waves crash against the shore in the distance. She paused at an open door to admire the view a few feet away from her. The warm glow of the scorching afternoon was abating, and a cool breeze rippled in from the beach. Isabel felt a sense of tranquility envelope her, and she let out a long sigh as her frazzled mind replayed the heated conversation she had endured with her parents.

Despite the weariness of the emotionally draining argument, she felt a flicker of hope ignite in her heart as she contemplated all that was said. It was the first time that her parents had taken her seriously enough to listen to her view. Her father had helped to keep her mother silent long enough for this to happen, but she felt as though an unsteady bridge had been patched up between them. She could feel her heart venturing along the rickety planks, reaching out to her mother and father on the other side.

Isabel smiled at the view.

"Can I help you?" an official-looking woman asked.

She wore striking red lipstick, and her thick black hair was in a tight bun on top of her head. She wore a fitted black evening dress and a red hibiscus flower in her hair.

"Sorry, I was just looking for the restroom and got distracted by the view here," Isabel explained.

"It is impressive, isn't it," the woman remarked. "I work here every day and still look longingly out of my office window for most of the day."

"Is this your resort?"

"Yes," the woman delivered a dazzling smile. "Though its success is largely due to the spectacular location."

"Kendra Waters?" Isabel inquired politely. "I'm Isabel Austin. My friend Rachel, the detective from the mainland, organized our stay here."

"Yes, I wanted to come and introduce myself, but your family seemed to be having a little tiff," Kendra explained with a tight smile.

"Sorry about that. I haven't seen my parents in a while, and I had to introduce them to my first boyfriend ever. I think that's why Rachel sent us out here, so that if there were any casualties, she wouldn't have to deal with them."

A tinkle of polite laughter escaped Kendra. "No, that can't be it. The island still falls under the mainland's police jurisdiction. Anyway, I think your main course has just gone out, so please enjoy the food, and call on me if you have any problems."

Isabel said her goodbyes and then hurried to the restroom. By the time she returned to the table, her mother's unmistakably obnoxious voice shattered the peaceful ambiance of the seaside evening.

"There is not enough spice in this dish," she insisted, sliding it forcefully away from her.

"You asked for the non-spicy version," a trembling Ross said, attempting to allay the fuming Colleen.

"That's preposterous," Colleen objected. "Why would I do such a thing?"

"I heard you ask for the non-spicy option," Isabel stated pointedly. "So please leave the waiter alone."

"I'm not so sure, Izzie, I think your mother ordered spice," Robert said, leaping in to defend his beloved wife.

"No matter," Ross apologized. He swiped a hand across his sweating forehead and removed the offending plate. "I will ask chef to prepare the correct meal for you."

Colleen gave an approving nod and Isabel sank mortified into her chair next to Ricardo.

"When I left, it was peaceful," Isabel muttered at him. "What happened?"

"Your father brought up the war," he hissed in her ear, "and let's just say my opinions didn't quite agree with your mother's."

"Sorry, I should've warned you," Isabel said, stifling a giggle.

Minutes later, an even more red-faced and sweating Ross delivered a second dish to the table. Isabel could smell the fiery spices from her seat.

"I hope this is more to your liking, ma'am," he said, apologizing profusely.

Colleen thanked him and Isabel watched as he darted away. The redhead seemed to be laughing at him. Isabel caught her eye for a moment and then looked away.

Her mother had managed a few mouthfuls before she began fanning her lips with waving fingers.

"Is everything alright, this evening?" the redhead asked after approaching the table.

"Everything is fine -" Robert began before his wife cut him off.

"Absolutely not," Colleen blurted, her cheeks a fiery red and her forehead glistening with sweat. "I think the chef is trying to kill me."

The redhead froze. "My name is Sarah, and I'm the manager here at the resort restaurant. Is there something I can do to help? Perhaps another meal."

Colleen was shaking her head furiously. "No, no, that bumbling waiter has already tried to bring me a different meal, and I'm convinced the pathetic excuse for a chef is trying to poison me with punishment."

Sarah smiled primly and Isabel noticed her pale hands clench and unclench behind her back.

"Chef Fabian is a world-renowned chef who graces our kitchen with his presence."

"I don't care if he's the chef at Buckingham Palace," Colleen interrupted. "I'm telling you this meal is an abomination."

"Mom, just order something else," Isabel pushed. "People are staring… again."

Colleen waved a dismissive hand. "I don't care. This isn't right, and someone needs to talk to the chef."

"No," Isabel groaned, her head sinking into her hands.

"Let me have a word," Ricardo suggested quickly, half rising from his chair.

"Not a chance," Colleen snapped at him. "You were against the war. And you call yourself a patriot. Ms. Sarah, please send for chef Fabio immediately."

Sarah hovered for a moment longer, the panic clear in her eyes. Colleen ruthlessly stared her down until Sarah timidly submitted and hurried away, her hands self-consciously wringing inside themselves.

"We're here on a favor from a friend," Isabel reminded her mother. "Do we really have to cause such a spectacle?"

"You were the one who said you wanted to learn how to stand up for yourself," her mother retorted with a familiar click of her tongue. "Well, I feel the need to teach you how to do it."

"Who complained about my food?" a heavily accented voice boomed from the kitchen door.

Knives and forks clattered on the plate as the diners jumped in fright. Eyes darted at the tall, hulking figure of a man in a chef's jacket as he stalked between the tables, his dark, beady eyes scanning the room for the guilty party.

Colleen Austin was not one to shrink back in fear. She raised her pudgy hand and waved it so that her glossy red nails would catch his attention.

"I have a complaint," she piped up.

Fabian homed in on her like a bull targeting a red waving flag. He barged past the tables and stationed himself in a heaving mass in front of her, his nostrils flaring wildly with every breath.

"And what is your complaint, exactly?" he forced out the words despite a clenched jaw.

"This is too hot. First you get my order wrong, and now you send this out. I'm very disappointed with the standard of food here."

Isabel wanted to hide under the table. Every morsel that had entered her mouth had even surpassed Ricardo's fine cooking, not to mention her mother's stodgy meals.

Fabian glared at her, his face reddening with fury rather than embarrassment. He launched towards her, and Isabel thought he might strike her mother, but instead he snatched a silver spoon from their table. The chef shoved the spoon into the contents of Colleen's meal, scooped up a decent portion, and lapped it up into his mouth, the food disappearing quickly under his impressive mustache.

"This is," he paused and thrust the spoon onto the table, "delicious."

Colleen looked as though she was about to pass out from an aneurism.

"How dare you stick your spoon into my meal!" she snapped at him. "I have never been treated so rudely before!"

"No time for this!" Fabian barked at her, his bristly eyebrows wiggling as he spoke.

He glared at her a last time before whipping round on his heel and marching back to the kitchen. Colleen remained seated, her face pale from the shock of being to publicly dismissed.

"Perhaps we should continue our meal on the beach," Ricardo suggested weakly. Isabel could tell that even he was tinged pink with embarrassment.

"No." Colleen shook her head resolutely as she squared her shoulders.

"Don't do it, love. Just let it go," Robert cautioned her.

"Are you going to let him talk to me like that?" Colleen demanded of her husband.

"I'm a nobody, darling, and I'm not about to make a name for myself by attacking the reputation of a famous chef!"

"Well," she shook her fist at him and heaved herself off her chair, "I can see where your loyalties lie. I think Isabel gets her weak nature from you!"

"Hey!" Isabel protested at the insult. "I enjoy having Dad's nature, thank you very much."

Robert retreated into himself. He picked up his fork and continued to poke at his delicious, herb encrusted lamb shank, though he looked as though he had lost much of his appetite.

"I'm going to sort this out myself," Colleen informed them primly before heading off in the kitchen's direction.

"Dad!" Isabel pleaded. "Aren't you going to stop her?"

"I learned a long time ago that there is no stopping your mother once she's set her mind to something."

"And just when I thought we were making progress as a family!" Isabel remarked sadly. "Mom is out of control!"

"What do you expect me to do?" Robert asked desperately. "You know what your mother's like!"

Isabel stood up. "Well, I guess then I'll have to be the voice of reason from now on."

"Isabel, wait," Ricardo begged, but she ignored him too.

With every step, Isabel felt herself become more uncertain. How was she to tackle her mother, as well as a ferocious chef who looked like he would throw her on a chopping board without a second thought?

"You can do this," Isabel whispered to herself.

She reached the staff entrance to the kitchen, heard bellowing from inside, and almost chickened out immediately. She bobbed on her heels, summoning courage from the buzzing air around her, and pushed into the kitchen.

Isabel was greeted immediately with a hot bustling kitchen, and they nearly knocked her over several times before she made her way to the safety of a wall.

"Excuse me... sorry!" Isabel tried to stop some cooks and waiters in vain.

"What are you doing in here?" Ross demanded, his voice a frantic squeak.

Isabel noticed his jacket was askew and one of his buttons was missing. He looked on edge after serving their table, and seeing a customer in the kitchen was enough to rattle him further.

"I'm looking for chef Fabian," Isabel stated determinedly. "My mother is trying to put him in the grave for her spicy dish and I'm hoping to intervene. I am sorry for all the disruption our table has caused you."

He scowled at her slightly, but gave an accepting nod to her apology. "I think I saw him going into the pantry for a breather."

Isabel thanked the surly waiter and made her way through the hive of activity in the kitchen. They greeted her with the most delectable smells and sights, and she had almost become lost in a world of culinary sensory overload when a piercing scream cut through the bubbly din.

Isabel recognized her mother's voice immediately. She had been shouted at enough as a child to pick that voice out from a stadium of world cup screams.

"Mom!" Isabel shouted in response.

The entire kitchen around her had frozen, though the pots and pans continued to boil and bubble intensely. Shouts of panic flew around as the chefs slowly returned to life. Hands stirred pots and wrists whipped away furiously at custard. Isabel pushed through the unnerved crowd towards what looked like the back section of the kitchen.

Isabel could hear a woman's voice blabbering in terror as she approached the storeroom door. She closed her eyes, her heart throbbing against her chest, and pushed through the door.

"Iz," her mother gasped in relief.

Isabel opened her eyes and found her mother trembling in front of her. Colleen's face was deathly pale, and she stared blankly at Isabel, her hands slowly raising from her sides and turning up. Isabel glanced down and recoiled at the red that stained her mother's hands, as though she had sliced up a hundred beetroots.

"What happened," Isabel tried to say, but her voice got stuck in her throat.

Her eyes had continued on their journey from her mother's face to her mother's hands, to the floor that was bathed in more beetroot juice.

Chef Fabian lay on his back at Colleen's feet. His white chef's jacket was drenched in blood. A glint of a silver hilt revealed the instrument of his death.

A carving knife.

"Alright, tell me what you saw one more time," Ricardo instructed in his gentlest of voices.

He had Isabel wrapped in a blanket and the resort medic was administering some calming pills so that she could talk properly.

Isabel related the scene once again. "My mother. Fabian. The knife. Is he?"

"I'm afraid so."

"And my mother?"

"You know how it works."

"Suspect?"

"Yes."

"I don't think she did it."

"Of course *you* don't. The entire kitchen staff does."

"I want the whiskey," Isabel mumbled.

The medic gave Ricardo a wary look.

"Not a chance," Ricardo smiled and smoothed his hands down her arms. "Remember what happened the last time you tripped over a body, and I innocently gave you some whiskey?"

"Bliss," Isabel recalled.

"No, you were drunk in seconds because your alcohol tolerance level is less than zero. You were hungover for days, and I can't have that happening again on my watch."

"Why not?" Isabel mumbled sadly. "It will help with the pain."

"Because more than ever, I need you to have your wits about you and help me solve this case. Can you do that?" Ricardo asked as he gazed intently into her eyes.

"I think so," Isabel nodded. "If it means proving my mother is not a murderer, then I guess I have to do what I can."

"There's my girl," he smiled.

"Can I see my mom?" Isabel asked weakly.

Ricardo hesitated and then finally agreed. "I'll take you to her."

He walked her down a quiet passage that led away from the noise of the restaurant.

"What's going on in there?" Isabel asked.

"The police arrived. They are separating people into groups and questioning them. No one leaves at this stage. The restaurant, and likely the entire resort, has been put under lockdown."

They reached a secluded door, and Ricardo tapped on it before entering. The argument inside was too heated for anyone to hear the polite knock.

"You were seen fighting with him," Rachel stated, "and then minutes later he turns up with a knife in his chest."

"And you just assume that I'm responsible?"

"You were covered in blood," Rachel continued matter-of-factly. "Our prime witness can testify to that."

"And by 'prime witness', you mean my own daughter," Colleen snapped. "Well, here she is. Ready to send her mother to jail like she's always planned."

Rachel jerked in fright when she saw Isabel.

"What is she doing here?" she hissed angrily at Ricardo.

"It's her mother," Ricardo pointed out the obvious.

"She's too close to this case." Rachel shook her head. "We can't have her working it."

"I'm not sitting this one out," Isabel insisted boldly. "I want to question my mother."

"Absolutely not!" Rachel denied. "Your emotions are too involved."

"Please don't let her question me," Colleen begged. "She doesn't have the brains for this type of thing."

"I'm trying to help you!" Isabel snapped at her mother.

"Precisely why I can't let you question her." Rachel barred her from the desk.

"She will have me incarcerated!" Colleen wailed in an uncomfortable tone. "She believes I've been a terrible mother, and this is how she gets rid of me!"

"I will not send you to prison!" Isabel squawked. "I just want to talk things through!"

"Let her have a few minutes," Ricardo asked his partner. "Please," he implored.

"Fine, five minutes," Rachel replied before marching out of the room. The willingness of her stride suggested that a coffee run was likely the real reason for her consent.

Isabel sighed and slumped into the chair opposite her mother.

"So," her mother shifted uncomfortably, "this is a strange turn of events. You're in the interrogation seat for a change. I bet you've waited your whole life -"

"If you had just listened to me and not fought with the chef, we wouldn't be here."

"If the only reason you asked to be here was so that you could say you told me so, then there's not much point to this conversation," her mother replied prissily.

"You were covered in his blood," Isabel repeated the memory, her voice cracking as she leaned forward.

"I was trying to help him!" Colleen explained, as though it was the most obvious thing in the world. "I went into the kitchen and demanded to talk to him. I was told he was taking a break in the back of the kitchen, and so I followed him there. When I walked in, I saw him struggling on the floor. So, I screamed for help and ran to help him."

"You found him like that," Isabel repeated. "With a knife in his chest."

"Yes," Colleen confirmed.

"Did you see anyone else in the room?"

"My focus was on that horrible chef," Colleen answered. "To be honest, everything else blurred around me."

Isabel sank her face into her hands. "You promise you didn't do this?"

Colleen laughed coldly. "Of course not. I might not be the best mother on earth—you've made that very clear tonight—but I would kill no one."

"Okay," Isabel nodded. "I believe you. And for the record -"

Isabel's sentence was interrupted by the door bursting inwards. Her disgruntled and red-faced father fought his way in. A police officer chased him down and tackled him round the waist, which sent them both sliding across the plush carpet.

"Rob?" Colleen shrieked at her husband as he struggled under the weight of the officer.

Isabel watched as her mother leapt off her chair, waddled her way over to the wrestling pair, and began kicking at the policeman.

"Get off my husband, you beast!" she yelled at him.

"I did it!" her father yelled. "It was me. I killed the chef. Let my wife go!"

The policeman howled for mercy and tried to shield himself with his arm. Colleen's aim was atrocious, and she landed every third kick at her husband instead of the officer.

"Mr. Austin!" Ricardo shouted. "You're *not* the killer!"

"I am, I swear. I killed the chef!" he insisted in between squeaks of pain.

"Dad," Isabel said, pulling her mother off the policeman. "I'll believe you if you answer one question."

The officer relinquished his grip at Ricardo's command. Colleen was still determined to go for him, but Isabel held her hefty mother tightly.

"Tell us *how* you killed Fabian," Isabel asked simply.

A look of panic passed over her father's anxious face, and he scrunched his eyes shut.

"I went to talk to the chef after he insulted my wife. I slipped through the back way so that no one would see me," he began. "Then I took..." he paused and remained silent for some time, "a rope and lassoed it round his neck. We wrestled for some time, but I overpowered him."

"Then where did all the blood come from?" Isabel asked, her fingers tapping impatiently on her arm.

"Blood?" her father repeated the word in surprise. "Yes, there was lots of it. I found a gun in his pocket and shot him with it. That's right. It was all a bit confusing."

"Alright, Dad, you've proven one thing to us."

"What's that?" her father asked, looking hopeful.

"That you are, without a doubt, *not* the killer!" she stated forcefully.

"No!" he cried, his frame crumpling to the carpet in defeat. "I did it, not my sweet Colleen. She'd never harm anyone."

"I know that, Dad," Isabel assured him. "But I'd rather find the truth and put away the real killer, instead of my father who's trying to lie to protect my mom."

"Is that what this is?" Colleen asked, clearly startled by her husband's oddly romantic gesture.

Robert turned distraught eyes on his wife. "I didn't know how else to save you, my sweet."

Colleen beheld him for a second longer and then launched her large frame at him, enveloping him in herself.

"I love you, my bear," she squeaked with delight in his ear before delivering a rather noisy kiss.

"Do you see why I need to be involved in this case?" Isabel pointed out to Ricardo and a shocked Rachel, who had just returned with a steaming mug of coffee.

Rachel nodded mutely, her face contorted with confusion as she tried to comprehend the bizarreness of the scene they had just witnessed.

"At least we can rule one suspect out with certainty," Ricardo agreed. "Robert was sitting at the table with me the entire time."

Chapter 5
The Italian Villagers

Isabel wound her way back to the restrooms. It seemed to be the only safe place to hide from interrogating officers, panicked diners, and fear-stricken staff members running around blindly and whispering in dark corners.

Isabel slumped her back against the cold, tiled wall and closed her eyes. She could hear the distant rumble of the ocean as nightfall settled on the remote island. Her mind conjured up the horrific bloody scene of her mother standing over the pale chef, her hands coated in the viscose liquid that shrieked of the pain and violence the chef had endured.

The silence of the restroom became oppressive, and she had the sudden urge to be closer to other living beings that could shield her from the horrors of an inexplicable murder. Isabel splashed her face with cold water, wiping off the miniscule amount of make-up she had been wearing, and wishing she could wash her memory clean as easily as her face.

She pushed her way out of the restroom and felt warmed by the noisy chattering of the waiting customers.

"It's been a strange evening," a voice found her.

Isabel jolted and turned to find the owner of the restaurant leaning against the wall with the painted mural splaying out around her.

"Does this happen often?"

Kendra laughed easily, though Isabel could see the tiny stress lines spidering out from her eyes.

"No," she shook her head. "We've never had a murder before. It seems almost surreal, as though we're trapped in one of those murder mystery movies, where no one knows who the killer is and so everyone is a suspect."

Isabel laughed. She could relate to the feeling. "Do *you* have any suspects?"

"What do you mean?" Kendra asked sharply.

"Someone stabbed your head chef in the chest with a chef's knife. That's quite a feat as chef Fabian was a large man. There was some force, some passion involved there."

"Are you implying that the murderer was someone on my staff?"

"I'm not implying anything, merely suggesting the possibility. Did Fabian have a troublesome time with your staff?"

Kendra looked away uncomfortably. "Fabian had a tough time with most people. He was not the easiest of people to get along with."

"Did he have any enemies?" Isabel pressed further.

Kendra thought for a moment, her features pensive. Isabel's eyes wandered over Kendra's shoulder to the colorful mural behind her. It depicted an Italian countryside vista, with warm fields dotted with red poppies. Two villagers kissed affectionately in the corner and a turquoise sea stained the background.

"His sous chef is probably at the top of the list," Kendra replied. "Fabian was a man whose reputation spoke volumes, and so many admired him. His under chef was the real faceless hero of the kitchen, compiling most of Fabian's dishes without a fraction of help. I think it wore Salvador down to see Fabian take all the glory for his hard work."

"That would gnaw away at anyone," Isabel remarked quietly, while her mind made a mental note to track down the sous chef and speak to him.

Kendra paused and surveyed her restaurant with a proud gleam in her eye, "I don't think Paul Salvador would dare raise a hand against his superior. He wants to advance up the food chain, but he wants to do it right. Then again, you never know what the drive for ambition can do to a person."

Isabel stored this information away for later use. "Was there anyone else in the restaurant who may have wanted to harm the victim?"

Kendra smirked. "You know very well I can't point fingers at my trusty staff members. What kind of example would I set as a loyal boss? I will tell you, however, to keep an eye out, and you should be able to figure it out yourself, without too much effort."

Isabel could not be entirely certain, but as Kendra turned to leave, Isabel swore her eyes flickered towards the colorfully painted scene behind her.

"This is quite an artwork," Isabel commented before Kendra could escape.

Kendra turned back and smiled, her hands folding across her chest. "Do you have some experience in the art field?"

"Yes, I run my little studio on shore. I also offer art lessons for the locals who want to learn."

"How adorable," Kendra remarked with the slightest hint of condescension. "What do you make of the painting on the wall behind me?"

Isabel bit her lip. She did not have time to offer her professional opinion on a restaurant mural, but she needed to keep Kendra Waters happy so that she would continue to allow Isabel to slip around her restaurant and question the guests.

"I wouldn't say a professional artist created it, but someone of a different trade, but with a hand in painting," Isabel remarked, noticing the subtle giveaways. "Over here, for example, the lines are rather amateurish, and the trees are a little out of proportion to the rest of the scene. But the painting is warm, inviting," Isabel paused, and allowed herself to absorb the peaceful scene, almost feeling the gentle sea breeze brush against her cheeks. "I love it," she concluded.

"I do too," Kendra smiled. "I can see we are quite similar in our tastes."

"I especially love the almost hidden couple in the corner over here," Isabel whispered. "They seem so undisturbed and in love."

"Yes, they're almost familiar," Kendra remarked with a knowing simper. She stepped closer and a glimmer of recognition flicked through her eyes as she studied the man and women.

Isabel noted the sleek red hair that hung elegantly down the painted woman's back, as the man, with a mop of messy brown hair, planted his lips on hers.

"Do you know the artist?" Isabel asked the unnecessary question. She could tell that Kendra knew exactly who had painted the mural.

"One of our waiters," Kendra replied. "Your waiter this evening, I believe."

Isabel recalled seeing the mopey waiter coming to life every time he and Sarah, the redheaded manageress, crossed paths. Observing the pair of them painted onto the restaurant's wall cemented his romantic intent. Isabel caught a flash of red, excused herself from Kendra, and followed the swish of auburn promptly.

Isabel tracked Sarah through the main dining room, which was crawling with anxious guests demanding to be set free from police observation. Sarah disappeared through a swing door and Isabel wasted no time pushing through herself.

To her surprise, she found herself in a small storage room packed to the brim with white tablecloths and napkins. Sarah's jacketed arm barred her path.

"Are you following me?" she demanded with an arced eyebrow.

"Yes," Isabel stammered the truth nervously.

The redhead was taller than her, and her high heels gave her a stilted height that made her appear even more intimidating in stature, though her rosy cheeks and hazel eyes were not threatening. Her lips were a perfect shade of tangerine to compliment her luscious locks.

"Why?"

"My mother is the prime suspect for killing the chef," Isabel explained awkwardly.

"So, you're looking for someone else to pin it on?" Sarah accused her, fear flashing through her eyes.

"I'm just looking to figure out some of the staff dynamics, and how they link to chef Fabian," Isabel explained as delicately as she could. "I wanted to ask about your relationship with -"

"So, you've heard already!" Sarah snapped, her eyes brimming with ready tears. "I knew the backstabbing staff would throw me out as the first suspect. Yes, I was in a relationship with Fabian, and no, I did not kill him! I hated him, but I'd never murder him like that."

Sarah withdrew into a corner, her shoulders shaking as she sobbed black mascara stains into a clean tablecloth. She pulled the sodden, stained white fabric away in horror.

"Ms. Waters will have me fired for this!" she sniffed. "I'll wash it before anyone finds out."

In a matter of seconds, and with only the prompting of a few innocent words, Sarah had crumbled, her outer shell falling away after a single attack.

"Sarah," Isabel stretched out a hand and laid it on the woman's trembling shoulder, her fingers smoothing down a loose thread that had been bothering her their entire conversation. "I didn't mean to -"

Sarah leapt away from her, her arms wrapping protectively around her tiny waist. Isabel was so stunned at the woman's reaction to a single touch, that she did not notice the door creak open, and another person step in behind her.

"What are you doing to her?" a man's voice demanded.

Isabel jumped and saw a seething Ross standing behind her, his face ghostly white and his dark hair a mess of curls.

"I was just talking to Sarah," Isabel explained, while still keeping an eye on the cowering Sarah. "I didn't want to hurt her, I swear."

"I think it's best you leave her alone," Ross ordered as he tried to shield Sarah with his own body.

"I just wanted to -" Isabel attempted again.

"I said leave!" Ross repeated loudly, causing Sarah to bury her face in his chest.

He had certainly stepped out of his constrictive role as a humble and obedient waiter, and assumed the position of Sarah's protector. Isabel wondered at the painted depiction of Ross and Sarah kissing on the restaurant mural, captured by Ross's own hand.

Isabel nodded and slowly retreated from the emotionally charged room, leaving Ross to comfort the grieving Sarah. She wondered why Sarah had remained in a relationship with Fabian, when it was perfectly clear that Ross was the one who openly adored her.

As Isabel walked through the packed dining room, she ducked to avoid being spotted by Rachel, who was busy pouring herself yet another cup of coffee. Isabel knew she needed to assemble the bizarre collection of clues she had absorbed since the moment she set foot inside the restaurant, which had shortly transformed into a gruesome murder scene. Isabel needed a quiet place to do this, and a hundred bulleted questions from Rachel would be too much to tolerate.

There were a few tables Isabel had to crawl under, and just when she thought she was finally free of Rachel, the detective strode past, the spikes of her heels missing Isabel's fingers by a hair's breadth. Isabel shrank under the table for a moment longer, before awkwardly leopard crawling into the kitchen. Safely inside, she leaned her back against the cold tiles and slid slowly to the ground, closing her eyes for just a second while her mind swam and her heart rate returned to normal.

"I see you needed an escape too," a low voice commented with a hint of amusement.

Isabel found a tall man staring down at her, his dark eyebrows practically knitting in the middle as he frowned. The corner of his long, thin mouth kicked up into a smile.

"S-sorry," Isabel stuttered, as she scrambled awkwardly up from the floor, finding herself out of place yet again. "I was just looking for somewhere quiet to think."

The man shook his head as if he understood. His white chef's jacket was unbuttoned at the top, revealing a healthy amount of chest hair poking out the top. His face relaxed, and he managed a weak smile.

"Would you like some coffee?" he asked calmly.

"That would be great," Isabel laughed gratefully. "I can tell by your jacket that you worked closely with Fabian."

"We are quite a number of chefs in this kitchen," the man explained. "How do you know I worked directly with him?"

"The fiery red sauce splashed onto your jacket is the same color as the main dish served to my mother. My guess is that you were the one, and not Fabian, who doctored her dish to try to satisfy her unreasonable request," Isabel observed.

The man held her in his blue gaze for a second, before cracking a wide toothed smile of disbelief. "You must be one of those investigators, although I think I saw you in the kitchen moments after they found chef Fabian dead. Who are you, exactly?"

"I'm Isabel," she replied. "And I'm just trying to figure out who killed your head chef so that my mother doesn't spend retirement in prison."

"You're a loving daughter," the man remarked, a glint of respect in his eyes. "I can't say I'd do the same for my mother."

"In reality, I fear she'd get murdered by her roommate, or possibly the other way round. My mother is not the easiest person to get along with," Isabel admitted with a guilty smile. "So, I'm not the wonderful daughter you imagine me, I just don't want blood on my hands."

"My name is Paul Salvador, and you're right. I worked directly under Fabian. It was a living nightmare I was only enduring with copious amounts of caffeine, and often something a little stronger," he admitted, his face souring.

He thrust a cup of coffee onto the counter, which Isabel picked up gratefully.

"It must be hard losing a coworker," Isabel offered.

"I think I'm still in shock," Paul said with a vague expression.

"Can you think of anyone who might have wanted him dead?"

"Apart from your mother?" he eyed her from under his bristly brows. "Plenty of people, myself included."

"You're very candid with that information," Isabel remarked, cradling her mug tighter. "There's an investigation going on, you know."

"It's not like you're the police," he laughed before studying her more closely. A doubt-filled frown crept onto his face. "You're not a cop, are you?"

"I'm not the police," she confirmed with a reassuring smile. "And you're not a murderer, are you?"

"No," he replied sadly. "I wanted to kill Fabian several times. I even daydreamed about how I would do it. Frying pan to the head, garlic butter and prawns everywhere. Not very exciting I know, but it seemed fitting enough."

"Not a knife to the chest?" Isabel asked sweetly, her big brown eyes watching every twitch of his face.

"I'm not a fan of blood," he explained with a grim shake of his head.

"You're a chef though," Isabel commented dryly. "Surely you're accustomed to blood and gore?"

"Only when it's a chicken, and it's already dead," Paul said with an almost laugh.

Isabel tried to subtly study the stains on his chef's jacket. She had assumed the blood-red drops were from the hot spicy sauce used in her mother's main course, but for a moment she wondered whether that was really so.

"I heard that Fabian was in a relationship," Isabel continued, deciding to see what other information she could glean from the talkative chef.

"Ah… poor, sweet Sarah," he remarked. "She must be happy he's no longer in the picture."

Isabel's face scrunched with confusion. A man was dead, and yet he was spoken about with so little affection by the very people that worked with him daily.

"Why didn't Sarah just leave Fabian if she didn't want to be in a relationship with him?"

Paul chuckled softly. "That's what we all said. I think Sarah tried to leave him a few times. I noticed the bruises for the first time a few months back. Sarah did her best to conceal them with make-up, but I grew up with an abusive father, so I know all the signs."

"Wait, you're saying Fabian hit Sarah?"

He nodded sadly. "For someone so observant, you sure didn't notice the obvious scars abuse leaves behind."

Isabel frowned. He was right. Thinking back, the signs were all there. Perhaps it was because she had grown up so sheltered and loved that she did not know what abuse really looked like.

"Why didn't she cry out for help?" Isabel asked, realizing it was a stupid question as soon as it left her mouth.

"And suffer a worse fate?" Paul shook his head. "I think Ross tried to get involved and help her, but it led to a rather nasty tussle in the kitchen between Fabian and Ross."

"So, Ross and Fabian had a history of fighting?" Isabel concluded.

"Kendra Waters, the owner, was furious. They knocked out an expensive oven the first time they fought. She pulled Ross from the kitchen and shoved him into the dining room as a waiter just to keep the pair of them separate. Although,

I think it was more to keep Ross from dying. He never won a single fight."

"Ross must have hated that," Isabel realized.

"See, it will not be so easy solving Fabian's murder," Paul pointed out, "because too many people wanted Fabian dead."

It was true. The list of suspects was growing. Isabel also had the distinct impression that everyone was trying to implicate someone else.

Paul disturbed her thoughts with one final slurp of his coffee mug. "Any more questions?"

"Just one. Who becomes head chef now?"

Paul squinted at her, his eyebrows joining in the center again.

"I do," he replied gruffly. "Now if you will excuse me, I need to see Kendra about that very subject."

Chapter 6
Amateur Sleuth

Isabel stayed a while in the empty kitchen, her mind continuing to whir through the range of suspects. She poured herself another mug of coffee and contemplated the plausible motives for each.

There was Ross. He had lost his position in the kitchen over a fight with Fabian. But she doubted Ross was a man of ambition. It appeared his genuine passion was for painting and love itself. Would a man like him be able to stand by and watch the woman he loved, Sarah, be thrown around by a brute like Fabian? Or would he step in and rescue her from her dire relationship, no matter the cost to himself?

Then there was Sarah. Confident manageress on the outside, but cursed by her own delicate nature and alluring looks that attracted a bully like Fabian. Once caught in his abusive trap, would Sarah eventually crack and lash out at the man who had hurt her emotionally and physically for so long? Sarah looked strong enough, and she was certainly tall enough, to wield a knife against Fabian, especially if she caught him by surprise. But Isabel doubted Sarah could mentally fight back.

And what about Paul Salvador, the overused sous chef who was forced to do all the hard work while Fabian claimed the fame? Perhaps the abuse over the years had been too much for Paul to endure, especially when Fabian's prestigious job was only inches away from his grasp. All he needed was a knife, fueled by ambitious intent, and a new job as head chef would be secured.

Isabel set down her mug, her eyes falling on a rack of knives. The chef's blade was missing from this set, and Isabel realized it was likely wrapped up in an evidence bag and labeled as the murder weapon. A shiver raked down her spine and she decided it was time to leave the vacant, brightly lit kitchen, which was now eerily devoid of the usual bustling activity.

A noise from the back thudded like a broom falling against the floor. Isabel jerked in fright. She had assumed she was alone. She held her breath, her ears straining for any sound of movement. She did not have to wait long, as something metallic, likely the lid of a pot, clanged against the floor.

Someone was definitely lurking around the kitchen, specifically, the crime scene.

Isabel imagined the murderer returning to get rid of some evidence the police had yet to discover.

She gnawed at her lip with her teeth, her hands wringing within themselves as she thought about what to do. She carefully slid off her shoes, and noiselessly approached the backroom, where she had found her mother wailing over the bloody figure of a once proud chef mere hours before. As she neared the door, she could hear definite signs of another person on the other side moving around.

Isabel took a breath and ducked under the yellow police tape that had cornered off the scene. She stood with her nose pressed against the door, a trembling hand resting on the handle as she worked up the courage to move forward.

Her mind flashed to her mother and the steady stream of accusations she had endured that afternoon about her general incapability at dealing with anything in life on her own. Her instinct was to run back and call Ricardo to her side, but Isabel knew that at some point she would have to progress through life without the help of her parents, or her best friend Delta, or her boyfriend, or even Rachel. Though she doubted life would be so cruel, that she would ever have to go on without the loyal, and very capable, help of her three fluff ball cats.

"Right," Isabel muttered to herself as her hand carefully pulled down on the door handle, "enough of this delay."

She cautiously pushed open the door, instantly aware that she could walk into a trap, designed by any of the potential killers, who were weary of her nagging and pointed questions. Isabel poked the top of her head through and felt the hair rise on the back of her neck and arms. She could see a jacketed man bent over double in a dark, back corner, as though examining something.

Isabel forced her entire body into the room, her buttons scraping against the wood. The man had not noticed her. Isabel stepped around the marked off outline of Fabian's body, gagging at the rust-colored stains on the tiled floor, and snuck behind a tower of crates containing vegetables. She crouched down and hid as much of herself as possible. Her hand brushed against something on the floor, and her fingers felt for the round object. Without removing her eyes from the man, she shoved the item into her pocket, reserved for later inspection. Likely a stray button, she thought to herself.

The man dragged a crate from the corner towards the outline of the body. He wore what appeared to be a brown potato sack over his head with two holes punctured for his eyes to see out. He drifted, like an old fuddy-duddy man trying to figure out his plan as he went.

Isabel watched the bizarre man bend stiff knees and scramble atop of the crate and stab into the air in front of him with his fist. She had seen enough. Murdering the chef was already a heinous crime, but returning to the scene to reenact it for simple pleasure was demented. He was clearly on a mission to destroy any kind of evidence left to find, and she would not allow it.

Isabel leapt out from behind her stack of crates and began hurling handfuls of globule-shaped sweet potatoes at him. The man grunted in pain as one bounced off his stomach. He doubled over and hobbled for cover. A rather large, sweet potato to the head knocked off his ridiculous make-shift balaclava, revealing a familiar face.

"Dad!" Isabel shrieked in shock. "What on earth are you doing here?"

He turned, his mouth agape and his eyebrows disappearing into his rugged hairline as he stared at her in shock.

"I might ask you the same question!" he snapped at her, a bruise forming on the corner of his head where he had been slapped with the tuber.

Isabel ran to his side, carefully skipping over chunks of potato. "I'm so sorry! I thought the killer was trying to destroy the murder scene or perform some kind of strange ritual. I wasn't sure."

"I was just trying to prove your mother's innocence," he admitted. "Seeing her in there…" a lump had formed in his throat. "She was so scared, so alone, and that awful lady detective was practically abusing her."

"From the looks of things, she was giving the detectives a harder time than they were giving her."

"I can't bear to lose her," he howled, burying his old face into her shoulder, "not after I've just lost you."

"You haven't lost me, Dad," Isabel replied glumly, her hand stroking his back awkwardly. "I've been here all along."

He drew away from her, his eyes blurred behind tears. "But you never visit. You never call. It's like you want nothing more to do with us."

Isabel felt shame rise from her heart and creep up into her cheeks, the heat causing her to flush.

"I'm sorry," she managed through a clogged throat. "I just needed some space from you both, and I didn't care how it affected you and Mom. But I can see how selfish I was being. I just so badly wanted to prove that I could do things on my own, and you guys never gave me the chance to do that. I was suffocating there."

Robert nodded slowly, as though he was trying to understand. "Well, you were pretty fearless coming in here and tackling me with all those potatoes. Weren't you scared?"

Isabel laughed through her own tears. "It terrified me. I think we might accomplish more if we work together. Two really amateur sleuths make a slightly more experienced one."

Her father's eyes lit up with a gleeful hope that she had not seen in a long time.

"Shall I explain to you the method of my madness?" he offered proudly.

"Please," Isabel urged him with another laugh.

"I was trying to figure out the height of the killer," her father explained, stepping back to the hideous outline of the chef.

"Fabian was a large man," Isabel recalled.

"Yes, the size of the outline confirms that," her father agreed. "And that's where I'm lost."

"Because Mom is so short?" Isabel guessed.

"Exactly," her father snapped his fingers and his eyes twinkled at her.

Isabel eyed the crate he had been using and realized what her father had been trying to achieve. She stepped closer to the murder scene. The high volume of blood was close to Fabian's chest area, and she remembered the knife sticking out of his left side, right where his heart would be.

"Mom would've been too short," she muttered to herself.

"I was trying to use the crate to get an idea of how tall the killer had to be to reach Fabian's upper chest area."

"You're a genius, Dad!" Isabel gasped. "I didn't think of this at all. They plunged the knife straight in, suggesting the killer was of equal height. Mom is far too tiny to have got the knife in herself."

"Unless she knocked him over first and then stabbed the knife into him?" her father suggested unwillingly.

"No, according to the blood patterns, Fabian was standing upright when he was stabbed. Fabian likely had his back to the killer, who crept up behind him and made an attack…" Isabel mused, trying to relive the order of events. "No," she corrected herself, "Fabian had turned to face his killer, again evidence that the killer wanted the chef to know who was bringing about his end. There was also a broken nose and some scratches which add to the confusion of his injuries," Isabel recalled.

"As emotionally strong as your mother is, I think that enormous chef would have just overpowered her in an instant. She may be round, but there is no strength in those muscles unless she is churning butter."

"I think this is enough to prove her innocence," Isabel clapped her hands. She paused and studied the smiling face of her father. "You know, you risked arrest… tampering with a murder scene… to prove Mom's innocence."

"Didn't you do the same?" he asked, with a spark in his eye.

"I guess I did," she laughed. "We both know Mom is no killer, unless it's the chickens roaming our backyard."

Her father laughed his easy laugh again, and Isabel felt like she was home on the couch watching television with him and scoffing a homemade slice of apple pie smothered in whipped cream.

"Let's talk to the detectives," Isabel suggested. "Then we can start looking for the real killer."

They turned to different exits and Isabel stopped.

"Wait, how did you get in here?" she asked.

"There's a hidden door in the back. You can enter the kitchen from one storeroom outside," Robert explained.

"So, the killer could've entered undetected, while everyone else was in the kitchen," Isabel realized. "It could literally be anyone then, not just people that were seen in the kitchen. That explains why Mom didn't bump into the killer on the way out when she came to help Fabian."

Isabel was still examining the location of the hidden door when the main entrance pushed open, and Paul Salvador stepped inside.

The expression on his dark face implied that his conversation with Kendra about his new job had not gone well. He offered the pair of them a ferocious scowl and demanded that they leave immediately.

"You're contaminating the evidence," he spewed at them as they hurried out the kitchen. "Apart from the fact that this is *my* kitchen, and you are trespassing!"

"One might ask what *you* are planning to do in there?" Robert shouted back, mustering up as much courage as he could.

Isabel watched as Paul towered over her father, his muscular arms hanging at his sides.

"You're quite tall, Paul," Isabel noted, distracting Paul from the easier target of her old father. "Taller than Fabian?" she asked with a sly smile.

"A little," he replied gruffly, not catching her intended meaning.

"It took a tall, powerful person to kill Fabian," Isabel pointed out. If an officer caught you messing around the crime scene, it would raise a lot of questions. I will inform the detectives to place a guard outside so that no one, not even the owner of this kitchen, can tamper with evidence."

Paul glared at her, and Isabel knew immediately that she had lost an alliance in him. His honesty would close-up, and she would have to find clues the hard way.

"Perhaps I'll report *you* to the police for sneaking in here," Paul threatened.

"But how would you explain why you were checking out the murder scene?" Isabel posed the question carefully.

Paul understood the threat instantly. He glowered at her and stormed out the kitchen.

"He's one to watch," her father muttered at her.

"I'm afraid he's not the only one," Isabel replied quietly. "Let's go free Mom."

Chapter 7
Burn the Evidence

"Well," a huffing Colleen spat, "I told you I was innocent."

Rachel rolled her eyes discreetly and shook her head. "You also told us there was no moon landing."

Isabel widened her eyes and covered her face with her hands, terrified that her mother would begin the long debate again.

"Now, don't get me started–" Colleen attempted before Robert hustled her away from the detectives.

"She's quite something," Rachel chuckled. "She's got some real fire in her."

"Colleen reminds me of you," Ricardo pointed out with a half-smile.

"Oh, really?" Rachel asked. She tapped a finger to her lips as she thought. "I think I shall take that as a compliment. The real question is," she grinned at Ricardo, "can you handle having someone like me as your mother-in-law?"

Ricardo paled instantly, and he backed away from his partner. Isabel blushed profusely at the implication of her and Ricardo being married one day. She may have already designed her wedding dress, but that did not mean that she was at all expectant, nor hopeful, of a certain question.

"Thank you for tolerating my mother," Isabel managed after she had regained control of her face.

"We might give each other hassle," Rachel explained, "but the old bat and I actually got on well."

"Like two peas in a pod," Ricardo added. "They were a fearsome duo. Thank goodness your mother never considered becoming a homicide detective."

"Well, maybe if I was as bold as you, my mother would approve of me a little more," Isabel muttered, more to herself than to her two friends.

"You're kidding, right?" Rachel said, taking her by the shoulders and shaking her. "Your mother couldn't stop raving about your successful art school and how you're the next big thing to hit FaceTube."

Ricardo snorted with laughter and Isabel found a lump wedge in her throat at the thought of her difficult mother being proud of anything she did. Isabel was not entirely sure what 'FaceTube' was, but she would gladly accept the compliment, regardless.

"You're more like your father," Rachel continued, unperturbed by Isabel's tears. "Soft hearted, but a real genuine soul that will do anything to help others in need."

Ricardo slung an arm around Isabel's shoulders. He knew her well enough to recognize the well of tears before they sprang.

"So, what's the plan now?" he asked Rachel.

"Coffee break," Rachel insisted. "Then we can discuss the progress of the case."

"I have a few suspects for you, though I want to investigate them a little more myself, before wasting your time with false leads," Isabel explained.

"Perhaps I could tag along for a bit, while Rachel gets more coffee?" Ricardo suggested.

Isabel felt the need to resist, though she could not quite explain why.

"Don't take this the wrong way," she began apologetically, "but earlier, when my dad and I figured out that my mother was innocent, it was... kind of... fun."

"Fun?" Ricardo repeated in disbelief.

"Yeah, like it was the first time I bonded with my dad over something. I think I want to ask him to do some more digging with me."

"It appears you're more alike than you ever thought," Ricardo pointed out. He stooped and kissed her on the cheek. "Let me know when you need some help."

"You absolutely cannot eat that," Colleen snipped at her husband.

"Darling, after all that brain work, I'm hungry. Besides, you offed the chef before we could enjoy our meal," he teased, "so I'm positively starving!"

Colleen snorted her pig-like laugh and slapped him playfully across the shoulder with the back of her hand.

"Dad," Isabel approached tentatively.

"Yes, dear," Robert said automatically, looking up and smiling at his daughter.

"Do you think you could help me figure out this case?" Isabel stammered through the question, as though she was sixteen, and asking for her father's permission to bring a boy home. "I mean, I know we proved mom's innocence, but I thought maybe if we pushed on, we might catch the actual killer, and that could be kind of... cool?"

Robert beamed at her as though she had just asked him to walk down the aisle with her.

"Of course," he agreed readily, with a warmth in his voice that Isabel savored.

Her mother cleared her throat noisily. "*I'm* the one who was falsely accused. I've only just been freed, you know. I might like a little quality time with my long, lost daughter too."

"I know, my dear, but this is something I'd like to do with our daughter, especially considering we have so little time together."

"I agree," Colleen sniffed. "My only complaint," she flicked her hair, "is that *I* was not invited on this little adventure."

Isabel's smile faded. Catching a killer with her father, who had already proved himself useful in finding clues, was one thing, but inviting her know-it-all, indiscreet, and domineering mother on her covert operation was another ordeal entirely.

"My love," Robert said gently, as he took his wife in his arms, "this is something I'd like to do with our little girl. It's not that we're excluding you, it's just that -"

"Three's a crowd?" she completed his sentence with a sorrowful expression.

He nodded sadly.

"Well, alright then. But you owe me," Colleen informed them.

"I promise I'll visit over the holidays for a week," Isabel conceded.

"Two," her mother negotiated expertly with a prim smile.

"Fine," Isabel grinned. She pecked her mother on the cheek and bounded off with her father, refusing to look back at the wounded puppy dog they had left behind. That particular expression had manipulated her often enough to have built up a resilience. "She'll be okay," she assured her father, after she felt him wavering after just one backward glance.

"So, what is the plan anyway?"

"I have three potential suspects in mind, though really anyone could've done it," Isabel said quietly, as they slipped out the door while the officers on guard were distracted.

"Who shall we investigate first?"

"I was thinking Ross, our waiter, but Paul's attempt to sneak back to the murder scene has pushed him up to the top of the list."

"How do we find more clues?"

"His locker," Isabel replied with a smirk. "What better place to keep your secrets hidden?"

"I spoke to some of his colleagues when I was trying to prove your mother innocent," Robert explained. "And they hinted at a few violent fights breaking out in the kitchen between Fabian and Paul."

"Really?" Isabel was shocked. Not only that Paul had eliminated that information from his interview with her, but more that her father had uncovered yet another fact she had not. "Paul mentioned nothing to me."

Her father winked at her as though he had far more tricks up his sleeve.

Isabel scouted for staff members who might lurk around the dark passageway between the kitchen and the staff locker room. They crept through the shadows until they reached the door and cautiously made their way through.

The room was empty. Isabel and her father split up so that they could try to locate Paul Salvador's locker faster.

"I bet you a chocolate brownie I'll find his locker first," her father hissed from behind a wall of lockers.

Isabel snorted. "You're on, old man. Lucky for me, you forgot your glasses," she added, noting the small lettering of the labels printed on each locker.

They both rounded the final aisle of lockers and, upon arriving at the same locker, shouted gleefully that they had each found it first.

"You just followed me!" Isabel accused him cheerfully.

"Are you calling your own father a cheat?"

"I am! I know the only reason mom won Monopoly our entire childhood was because you were sliding money out of the bank and into her stash!"

Her father stared at her in shock. "You were clearly an investigator your whole life. But I've got one last test for you."

"Name it."

"How did your brother's pet hamster really die?"

"Mom sat on him while eating a donut," Isabel replied with a wave of her hand. "That was easy."

"But," he spluttered, "how could you have possibly known that?"

"I found the dress she'd been wearing in the trash with a rather oddly shaped stain, and the one couch cushion was lighter than the others, suggesting it had been washed."

"You're a genius. Now tell me, how do we get into this locker?"

Isabel thumped her fist into the top left corner and the door swung open. Her father's jaw dropped as though he had just witnessed the ultimate magic trick.

"How..." he stammered.

"My dear older brother always hid my locker key so that I wouldn't have my books for class -"

"Your brother would never do such a thing," her father instantly defended their golden boy.

"I think I've already proven myself the family investigator. Anyway, I developed this trick in high school. It jolts the latch inside and it unlocks on its own."

"Genius," he murmured, his expression one of awe.

"Right, let's see what we have," Isabel said while shining the flashlight on her phone into the dark space. "Change of clothes, shoes, shower gel, a self-compiled recipe book... wait," Isabel paused and pulled the recipe book out. "Not just recipes, it seems."

"What did you find?"

"A bunch of official looking letters from Kendra Waters."

"What do they say?" her father asked over her shoulder, his old eyes squinting at the tiny font.

"This one says that the resort rejects Paul Salvador's claims to have Fabian removed as the head chef here. Kendra claims there is not enough evidence, and that removing Fabian would unsettle the restaurant and the staff.

Kendra also explains that Fabian was chosen for his reputation and the fame attached to his name, and not for his skill in the kitchen. She says that if she could, she would gladly get rid of him, but they were stuck in a three-year contract."

"Wait, who's this Kendra?" her father asked in confusion.

"She owns this establishment. So, I guess she has a big say in who gets hired."

"She doesn't appear to like our murder victim very much," her father observed.

"I agree with you. This letter gives the impression that Kendra felt Fabian was more trouble than he was worth."

"The sous chef must have been furious when he read that all his hard work would continue to pump up the reputation of his rival, and boss in the kitchen."

"I agree with you. This is definitely worth pointing out to the detectives."

"Do you think Fabian had a locker in here?"

"The police would've cleared it already. Paul's was untouched because he's not an official suspect -" Isabel froze mid-sentence, her whole body alert.

"Wha -" he began before Isabel pushed her hand over her father's mouth so that it silenced him.

The door squeaked open, and they could hear footsteps. It sounded like a pair of high heels clacking against the floor, though the occupant was clearly trying to make as little noise as possible.

Isabel signaled her father to stay where he was, while she crept forward to try glimpse their surprise visitor. They could hear metal clanking against the ground, as though a trashcan was being dragged out.

All Isabel could see around the edge of the lockers was a pair of hands tossing clothes into the trashcan. It looked like one of the staff uniforms, though Isabel could not be certain from her distance. Next, Isabel heard the distinct sound of a match being struck.

"She's burning evidence," Isabel hissed to herself. "Stop!" she shouted, before springing out from behind the lockers.

Over the smoking crackle of fabric, Isabel could hear the thudding of high-heeled shoes charging out the door, followed by a high-pitched shriek and the slosh of water. She was too busy dealing with the smoking pile of material in the trashcan to worry about the woman. After a few burnt fingers, Isabel hauled the clothes out of the trash. Once on the floor, Isabel melted the soles of her shoes stamping out the flames.

The result was a flaming trashcan behind her, and heavily smoking clothes at her feet. Another slosh of water behind her put out the flames, and Isabel spun round to discover her mother proudly clutching an empty bucket to her chest.

"What are you doing here?"

"I followed you," Colleen stated with a grin.

"I told you to stay away. You just cause trouble!"

"I think, this time, that you really needed my help," her mother claimed defensively. "I helped you catch the person running away."

"I don't see her," Isabel pointed out, with a hand on her hip. "Do you know who she was or what she looked like?"

"No, it was dark in the hallway, and she was too fast."

"Then how did you help exactly?" Isabel asked, folding her arms across her chest.

"Well," her mother huffed, "for a start, I put out the fire in the trashcan you ignored. And second, I slowed down the runner."

"How?" Isabel asked doubtfully.

"No time for that," Robert interrupted. "Grab your evidence and let's get out of here. I suspect it triggered an alarm with all this smoke."

Isabel picked up the tattered pieces of fabric and had just pushed through the door when she bumped straight into an unyielding frame. It felt as though she had walked into a steel wall.

She looked up slowly and gulped in response to the fierce blue scowl that met her eyes.

"Paul," she managed. "We were just leaving!"

"I bet you were," he yelled at her as she hurried past him and out of arm's reach. "I'm going to press charges against you!" Paul shouted after them.

"He's rather terrifying," her mother puffed as she waddled behind them. "Seems like the murderer to me."

"I don't think murderers go around pressing charges," Isabel pointed out. "Let's hide in here."

They tried the unlocked door and found themselves in a well-lit and quiet storeroom.

"So, what did you rescue?" her father asked curiously.

"A uniform. A lot of damage was done, but judging by the red smudge on the collar, I'd say this belongs to a woman."

"Why would someone want to get rid of their uniform?" Colleen asked.

"Perhaps it was what the killer was wearing when she attacked Fabian. Maybe there was a trace of blood, or something that could prove our killer guilty," Isabel reasoned while she carefully searched through the singed pockets and folds of fabric.

"Any clues?" her mother asked, unable to contain her excitement.

"What were you doing there?" Isabel asked again.

"I told you, I wanted to see what you and your father were up to," Colleen explained, her cheeks pink from the excitement.

"You couldn't bare not to be included," Isabel accused her. "This was something Dad and I were doing."

"I know," her mother looked guiltily at her shoes. "I tried to respect that, but I was jealous that you wanted to spend time with him and not me. I also wanted to see what you're capable of. And seeing you in action…"

Isabel braced herself for the criticism.

"I'm…" she struggled for the right word, "impressed, my darling girl. You're not the scared, useless girl who could not even fry an egg. You took charge, and you were, dare I say, braver than I've ever been," Colleen got the words out, though her voice was wobbly, and tears threatened to rain down at any moment.

"Mom…" Isabel gasped, surprised at the how hard she had to fight to suppress her tears. "I still can't fry an egg, but I've learned to do many other things."

Isabel was so unaccustomed to hearing her mother compliment her she did not know how to respond appropriately.

"We're very proud of you," Robert grunted with a quick swipe of his hand to his eyes.

"No," Isabel shook her head, not allowing herself to accept the compliment. "I put you and Mom in danger. There's a killer on the loose, and something bad could've happened to both of you."

"Your father and I feel younger than we've felt in years," Colleen laughed. "Now, we've got a killer to catch. Did you find any clues?" her mother asked with genuine interest written on her face.

Isabel jumped back into action. She worked carefully with the scorched fabric. The fire had already damaged the evidence and she certainly did not want to be responsible for losing any more forensic clues. Rachel would have her sit a night in jail if she did.

"I see you've been busy," Ricardo's voice echoed around the empty room.

"You got my text," Isabel said with a smile.

"I did. And I think I caught the person responsible for setting the uniform on fire," Ricardo added with a grin.

"Who?"

"Sarah Webber, the victim's girlfriend. She's with Rachel now."

"Sarah! How did you know it was her?"

"They drenched her to the bone," Ricardo explained. "Someone must have thrown a bucket of water at her."

Colleen winked at her daughter. "I told you I'd come in handy."

Isabel wrapped an arm around her mother's wide waist and gave her a squeeze. Still shaking her head with disbelief, Isabel turned her attention back to the blackened uniform.

"Wait," she paused, her eye caching an unusual patch of color amidst the black and white. "What color does this look like to you?"

The two men in the group shrugged, as though they had been asked a bizarre question. "Red?" they both responded.

"Tangerine," Isabel corrected them. "There's a little more orange to the shade. And can anyone tell me which of the female staff was wearing this shade of lipstick?"

Again, the men were baffled by the question.

"The owner, Kendra Waters, was wearing red lipstick," Ricardo replied confidently.

"Correct," Isabel agreed, "Kendra is indeed wearing red lipstick, but this," Isabel gestured to the smudge on the white shirt, "is not red. It's tangerine."

"Sarah wore that shade, if I'm not mistaken," Colleen pointed out.

"And you must be where I get my artist's eye for color from," Isabel grinned at her mother, surprised at how much they really had in common. "Sarah was wearing this precise shade."

"So, then she was trying to burn her own uniform," Ricardo concluded. "She must have known that once we found out about her relationship with Fabian, we would suspect her."

"Women rarely stain their own uniforms with lipstick," Isabel remarked, her finger tapping against her chin while she thought. "There's a missing button, too. Anyway, the only way to find out is to talk to Sarah and ask her."

"Rachel is conducting the interview as we speak," Ricardo explained.

Isabel raised an eyebrow and suppressed an icy shiver. "Then we don't have a moment to lose."

Chapter 8
Facing the Past

"Just tell me why you set a pile of evidence on fire you blasted murderer!" Rachel was yelling at a trembling Sarah.

Sarah wailed an unintelligible sentence in response to the battering of questions.

"Thank you, detective Taylor," Ricardo said calmly. "I will take it from here."

Rachel's face reddened, and she glared at her partner. Isabel offered her raging friend a steaming cappuccino as a peace offering.

"I have her at breaking point and you come in and interrupt!" Rachel hissed at them.

"You're aware Sarah was in an abusive relationship with Fabian, right?" Isabel asked her quietly so that Sarah would not overhear.

Rachel nodded, as if she did not gather the connection.

"So, Sarah is *always* at breaking point. Shouting at her is going to get you the answers you want, but not necessarily the truth."

Rachel groaned loudly and snatched the cup of coffee from Isabel. She stormed out of the room, leaving Isabel and Ricardo to deal with the wailing Sarah.

Sarah had mascara running down her cheeks and her tangerine lipstick was long gone. Her damp red hair pulled back into a ponytail and she sat shivering on a chair.

"Sarah," Isabel approached her carefully and set a second cup of coffee down on the table for her. "How are you?"

Sarah flicked her long ponytail over her shoulder and glared at Isabel. Isabel noticed that Sarah's clothes were still wet and clung to her. Ricardo gave her a nod and then stepped out of the room. He returned quickly with a police blanket, which he flapped out and wrapped around Sarah's shoulders.

"So, what happened down there?" Isabel asked gently, her hands slipping into her pockets.

"What, are you supposed to be the good cop act?" Sarah scoffed. She whipped away her tears with the corner of the blanket.

"I'm not a cop," Isabel corrected her. "I'm just trying to find out who killed Fabian."

"Why? Fabian was a terrible man. He deserved to die," Sarah replied ruthlessly, the emotion scraping her throat.

"Regardless," Ricardo intervened. "Murder is against the law."

"So is abuse!" Sarah fired back at him.

"Is that why you killed him?" Ricardo pressed, hoping the question would catch Sarah off guard.

"I didn't!" she cried. "But I knew the police would assume I was the killer," she continued, "that's why I burned my uniform."

"What were you trying to hide?" Isabel stepped into the interview again.

"I'd been in a fight with Fabian earlier today," Sarah explained, her trembling fingers swiping a tendril of hair out of her face. "I tried to break up with him again, and things got heated. He slapped me around a bit, and this time I fought back."

"Could you describe the fight in more detail," Ricardo requested gently.

"Fabian grabbed me around the neck. I couldn't breathe, but I struggled out of his grip and scratched him," Sarah said in a strangled voice.

"He can't hurt you anymore, Sarah," Isabel whispered. "It's safe to talk here."

"I was so angry, I struck him in the face," Sarah admitted. "For the first time. My fingers stung like crazy, and I could see the red stripes burn into his face, but I didn't care."

"That conforms to the coroner's report. They found scratch marks on the victim's hands and wrists, and there was slight bruising to the face."

"But I didn't kill him," Sarah stated resolutely. "I would never be strong enough to."

"What evidence do you think your uniform contained?" Isabel repeated the question.

"I thought there might be some drops of blood from Fabian."

"How did Ross react when he heard Fabian refused to let you leave him?" Isabel asked quietly, her eyes watching Sarah's pale face closely.

Sarah jolted at the sound of Ross's name.

"Uh..."

"You told him, of course," Isabel added quickly. Sarah was off guard.

Sarah could not stop the nod. "Yes, I told him."

"When?"

"When?" Sarah repeated, her mind in a daze.

"When did you and Fabian get into a fight?" Isabel clarified.

"Shortly before he died," Sarah explained.

"And when did you talk to Ross about it?"

"Immediately after," Sarah recalled, realizing that the timeline was adding up quickly.

"How did Ross react?" Isabel repeated her initial question after her trap had been successfully laid.

"He was…" Sarah hesitated and was clearly angry at herself for having been caught out. "Ross was furious," she admitted. "Understandably!"

"And?" Ricardo added. "What did he *do* after that?"

"I… I don't know," Sarah stammered, her eyes filling with tears again. "All I know is that this," she paused and threw off her blanket and unbuttoned the top of her jacket, "is what Fabian did to me."

Her neck was an array of fresh, painful bruises.

"I can show you more," she threatened, her eyes wild.

"I'm sorry you had to go through this," Isabel sympathized. "You know, sometimes I felt like I was stuck in an oppressive relationship with my family. I realize now that I do not know what you've been through. I cannot imagine how strong you've been to survive this long. I know I never would've been able to do. I'm sorry if these questions have been difficult to answer, but I'm really proud of you for getting through this interview." Isabel turned to Ricardo. "I think that's enough for now. Sarah, why don't you change into something warmer, and then begin your formal report for the police."

Sarah nodded gratefully, and Ricardo summoned a police officer to escort her. Ricardo offered Isabel a puzzled look.

"What's going through your mind?" he asked her.

"The scratches on Fabian," Isabel replied vaguely, her focus far away. "Did they draw blood?"

"No, they didn't break through all the layers of skin."

"And the slap to the face?"

"Again, there was only bruising. No blood. Why?"

"Then why would Sarah need to burn her uniform? The evidence would be under her nails, not on her clothes," Isabel pointed out.

She had paced the room and Ricardo was following her helplessly while he tried to keep up.

"Did you notice something familiar about what she was wearing?"

"She was in another resort uniform?" Ricardo guessed.

"Not quite," Isabel shook her head. "There was a loose thread on her shoulder when I spoke to her earlier this evening. It was still there when we interviewed her now."

"What are you implying?"

"Sarah Webber was not trying to burn her own uniform to conceal evidence. She was trying to cover up for someone else," Isabel concluded with a grave expression.

Ricardo stopped her in her tracks and gave her a spontaneous kiss.

"You're brilliant, Izzie," he whispered to her.

"I agree," her father's voice trembled behind them.

Isabel jumped a foot and found her mother and father watching the 'private' conversation she had been having with Ricardo.

"How did you get in here?" Isabel demanded, her face scarlet from being caught kissing a boy by her parents.

"We were listening in on your nice little chat with that sweet girl, you know, the one with all the bruises," Colleen explained without a trace of shame.

"You mean, you were spying on an active police case?" Ricardo said, suppressing a laugh.

"Is that illegal?" Colleen asked doubtfully. "It's a free country isn't it?"

"Don't worry," Ricardo laughed openly, "I will not press charges. It's just, I can see where your daughter gets it from."

"Me?" Isabel choked in horror.

"Yes, you," Ricardo said with a fond smile. "Your inquisitive nature drew you to our police cases. Your parents seem to share the same keen interest."

"Oh, Izzie," her mother slapped a hand playfully across her daughter's arm, "would it be so terrible to have something in common with us?"

Isabel chuckled along with the rest of her family. "I guess not," she agreed.

"Now, you were saying something about that Sarah girl burning evidence for someone else," Robert recollected. "Who do you think she was trying to cover up for?"

"I think I have a fairly good idea," Isabel said quietly, her fingers playing with the object in her pocket.

Chapter 9
Moonlit Confessions

"Looking for someone?" Isabel directed her words at the back of a messy head of dark hair.

Ross spun on his heel, a flicker of annoyance crossing his face when his eyes found hers.

"I was just wondering when we'd be allowed to leave this stupid restaurant and get back to our lives," Ross muttered at her.

"Sarah was saying much the same thing," Isabel said vaguely.

She watched Ross's face flood with relief. "You've seen her?"

"Yes, the police just finished interviewing her. Naturally, she's a suspect."

Ross turned stark white, and he had to swallow his shock before he could speak. "Why would she be a suspect?"

"I caught her burning her uniform," Isabel explained. "She claims she got into a big fight with her boyfriend, Fabian, just before he dropped dead. She even showed us the bruises. Sadly, it's a long shot to believe that she didn't take matters into her own hands and just stick a knife into his chest -"

"How dare you!" Ross bellowed at her. "Sarah is the sweetest, gentlest creature. She would harm no one, not even if it was in defense of her own life."

"Didn't she tell you?" Isabel gasped a little too dramatically. She could see her mother signaling for her to tone down her acting skills. "Sarah fought back. Fabian's autopsy report came through, identifying scratches on his arms and a bruised face -"

Ross gripped Isabel by the arm and dragged her to one door that exited onto the beach. The moon slashed across the silver crests of waves as they crashed violently against the shore. The chilly breeze that blew against her face was refreshing and helped sharpen Isabel's senses to the fact that she could potentially be dealing with a killer.

"Sarah fought back, but it was just this one time, and there's no way she killed him!"

"You can't be sure of that," Isabel insisted. "Sarah burned her uniform to hide Fabian's blood."

She watched the torment rip through Ross's dark features.

"Unless," Isabel dropped the word just before he broke, "Sarah wasn't burning her own uniform. You see," she fixed her eyes on Ross, "I noticed that Sarah's uniform didn't change. There was a loose thread that bugged me all afternoon, and it was still there even after she claimed to have changed."

"Our uniforms all look the same," Ross coughed.

"But yours doesn't," Isabel continued, disappointed that Ross had not taken the bait to clear Sarah's name. She pulled her hand out from her pocket and held out a single button. "Look familiar?"

Ross scowled at the button, his fingers running down the front of his jacket.

"It's a button from the standard issue uniform, so what?"

"I found it close to where Fabian was killed."

Ross paled again and his hand tremored slightly as it ran over the line of neat buttons. "As you can see, mine are all still intact."

"That's what doesn't quite make sense," Isabel continued relentlessly. "You see, I bumped into you on the way into the kitchen to find my mother, and you were on your way out. I remembered seeing your jacket disheveled and roughed up, as though you had been in a fight."

"It was hot in the kitchen, and I took my jacket off -"

"It was not until I inspected the jacket Sarah had tried to burn. It too, was missing a button. So, I don't think she was trying to burn her own uniform. I think she was trying to cover up for you."

Ross began backing away from her, his polished shoes sinking into the soft grass that encircled the beachfront restaurant. Lanterns twinkled around them, and the stars glittered above.

"Sarah told you she had been in a fight with Fabian, yet again, after trying to leave him. This time, you were going to do something about it," Isabel explained. "So, you stormed into the kitchen and took matters into your own hands. You confronted Fabian."

"Can you blame me?" Ross shouted at her. He was now standing on beach sand, his face hidden in shadow. "Fabian kept hurting the woman I loved, and he refused to let her go, even when she gave it her all to leave him! Why should he be allowed to keep her caged like a wounded animal? I had to do something."

"What did you do exactly, Ross?" Isabel asked the incriminating question.

"I pushed my way through that kitchen and found him in the back storeroom. He was cleaning the scratches on his arm. I told him Sarah was through with him and would move on."

"And?"

"And he laughed at me. He tried to walk away from me, but I -" The whites of Ross's eyes flashed wildly in the moonlight. "I just wanted him to leave Sarah alone."

"What did you do?" Isabel demanded.

Ross had backtracked further down the beach and Isabel could feel cold water lap at her toes. The smash of the waves against the shore almost drowned out Ross's words.

"I gave him a taste of his own medicine," Ross fired at her.

"With a knife."

"No!" Ross objected. "With my fists! I landed one right on his nose!" Ross explained gleefully. "It was the best moment of my life getting one back on a monster like him."

"But you couldn't stop there, could you?" Isabel pushed him a little further. "You had to show him what a real bully he was! And you didn't know how to stop," Isabel explained sadly.

Ross's eyes glistened wet in the moonlight. He turned away from her and stared out at the ocean.

"No," he said in a broken voice. "I wanted to kill him with all the strength I had, but it wasn't enough. I was too weak! I couldn't even defend myself, let alone the woman I wanted to call my own! I've never won a fight against Fabian."

Ross kicked out at an encroaching wave in frustration, sending a spray of salty water toward Isabel. She could feel the self-loathing washing off him. He seemed almost resentful that he was not the killer.

"I got in a punch or two, breaking his nose, and then Fabian gripped me around the neck."

Ross pulled open his jacket buttons to reveal invisible bruises to Isabel. She squinted at his throat but could see nothing in the darkness.

"As soon as I got out of his vice-grip, I bolted for the door, furious with myself, and embarrassed at my defeat. Fabian was still standing, gloating over his victory."

"Sarah burned your clothes to get rid of Fabian's blood from the broken nose," Isabel reasoned, the facts pulling together.

"I might not have killed Fabian, but I will be proud to go down for his murder," Ross stated boldly. "Just promise you won't tell Sarah the truth. I want her to believe that I rescued her from him."

"Ross, no, this makes little sense. Sarah could never love a killer. She was trying to escape one, so why would you want to become the very thing she was running away from?"

Ross shook his head, rejecting the world of reason she was appealing to, and choosing instead to fall back into his own world of delusional heroism. Despite the darkness, she could see the determination surge through his features and before she could do anything, he leapt away from her and ran back up the beach.

"I killed Fabian!" he shouted as he ran.

"No, Ross!" she shouted after him, losing him in the darkness.

The beach lit up with powerful torchlights in an instant, and police officers in reflector jackets leapt out from inside hammocks, behind palm trees, and portable minibars.

They swarmed along the beach, tracking the fleeing figure of Ross.

"Ricardo," Isabel called, grabbing onto a tall officer that looked like him.

"Sorry, ma'am," the strange officer replied with a wink.

Isabel scanned the blur of faces in the dark, unable to locate either Rachel or Ricardo. She kicked at the sand in frustration and stomped off back inside the restaurant.

"That was brilliant!" her parents saluted her as she entered.

"Why the glum face?" Robert asked her.

"I think we've got the wrong guy," Isabel explained with a scowl.

"But he confessed, we heard him!" Colleen squealed excitedly. "That useless waiter of ours shouted it for the world to hear."

"He also admitted not being able to go through with it because he was too weak," Isabel recalled.

Colleen and Robert frowned at each other. "We didn't hear that part. There was too much background noise to carry over your microphone."

"The waves," Isabel slapped a hand to her forehead. "He led me down to the water so that the crash of the waves would block out what he wanted to tell me!"

"I don't understand," Colleen said with a crinkle of her piglet nose.

"Ross wants to take the fall," Isabel explained, "so that he can feel like he rescued Sarah. This is terrible! The police will never believe he's innocent when he openly confesses."

"They didn't believe me when I confessed," Robert commented indignantly.

"That's because you had zero proof," Isabel laughed. "It was entertaining to watch though."

"Can't *you* disprove Ross as the killer?" Colleen asked innocently.

"The police will want to wrap up the case. Unless I can track down Rachel or Ricardo and beg them to hold up closing the case, things will move pretty rapidly from here."

"Then perhaps you will just have to try to catch the actual killer again," Robert suggested.

"I need to talk to Sarah," Isabel decided. She spun on her heel and marched straight into Kendra Waters.

"I believe I have you to thank," she said in a warm voice, "for catching Fabian's killer. I never would've believed Ross capable of murder."

"I'm not so sure he is," Isabel replied abruptly.

"On the contrary," Kendra disagreed. "Ross has been apprehended and is in the middle of a confession right now. I heard part of it myself. He took the knife from Paul's rack, followed Fabian into the backroom and ended things."

"He had it all worked out," Isabel noted. "You must be relieved, Mrs. Waters. Your restaurant and resort can go back to normal."

"No," Kendra shook her head, her hairdo and red lipstick still immaculate despite the grueling day, "my restaurant will be even better without the dark cloud Fabian cast over us with his brutish behavior and temperamental nature."

Isabel was saddened by the relief she could see on Kendra's tired face. One man's life meant so little in the grand scheme of things. The resolution of his murder simply meant that life could better continue without him. That was a tragic legacy to leave behind; one in which the world was easier without you.

"Thank you, Isabel Austin, for assisting the police in catching such a violent killer like Ross. Please know that you and your family are welcome to stay for the rest of the weekend, and all your meals and activities will be on the house."

Colleen and Robert were jumping up and down like five-year-old kids in a bouncy house.

"Thank you, that's most kind of you," Isabel said with a forced smile. "I really don't think Ross is the killer -"

"Leave policing to the police, dear. Now, if you'll excuse me, I have a ton of paperwork to sign off with the police."

Isabel watched as Kendra made her way out of the dining area. She passed a distraught Sarah, who was shuddering from head to toe and cradling what looked like a mug of port.

"Sarah?"

"Get away from me. I blame you for this! Ross is not the killer!"

"I know." Isabel dropped to her knees in front of Sarah. "I need your help."

"Look where that got me last time," Sarah growled at her.

"Did you see Ross changing uniforms?" Isabel threw the bizarre question at her.

Sarah tried to reorganize her muddled thoughts. She closed her eyes and nodded. "I did. He was rambling about wishing he'd been the one to kill Fabian."

"He said the same to me," Isabel explained in a low voice. "Is that why you stole his uniform?"

Sarah nodded. "I had a bad feeling that he was going to use it to implicate himself. Fabian's blood was on there, I don't know how, but it was."

It added up. Sarah had clearly not known about the broken nose, which was why she did not mention it when she tried to claim the uniform as her own.

"So, you knew he might do something rash, and you thought that by burning the evidence, you could put a stop to it," Isabel concluded.

Sarah nodded sadly. "I failed. This is all my fault. If I'd just tried harder to stand up for myself."

"Not necessarily, Sarah. Love is blind. My father tried to take the fall for my mother when she was the prime suspect in this case. Ross wants you to see him as the hero who saved you from the reaches of an overbearing boyfriend."

"He doesn't have to go down for murder for me to believe that," Sarah sobbed into her hands. "I already know it's true."

"Then I need you to help me prove his innocence. I'm going to ask you a series of questions," Isabel stated frankly, "and I need honest answers."

Sarah nodded quietly.

"When Ross was changing out of his uniform, did you notice anything on his body?"

Sarah thought back, her finger straying to her mouth. "He had red streaks around his neck, almost as though bruises were forming. They looked pretty similar to mine," she recalled. "And his hands were quite beat up too."

"Do you know what caused those marks on his neck?" Isabel pressed.

Sarah shrugged her shoulders. "He didn't say. I assumed it had to do with his fight with Fabian."

Isabel extended a hand and squeezed Sarah's arm. "We will prove Ross innocent, even if he claims he is guilty."

Sarah's eyes locked on hers and she mouthed the words, "Thank you."

Rachel strode into the room with an air of confidence wafting behind her. She looked exhausted. It was the early hours of Saturday morning and she had been covering a double shift all week. Dark rings encircled her eyes, and she gripped her twelfth cup of coffee. She was flanked by two equally exhausted officers.

"Right, gather round," she ordered everyone. "We have apprehended a suspect, and he offered a full confession. We have enough evidence to support his claims and so we will wrap up the case for now. You're all free to go to bed, but don't leave town."

There was an audible sigh of relief that circulated the room. Tired guests gathered up their expensive high heels and designer handbags and readied themselves to slog back to their rooms. Staff members staggered to their feet and ignored the heaps of dishes as they trudged towards their boss, Kendra, grimly aware that their next shift began in a matter of hours.

"Thank you, detectives," Kendra said as she shook Rachel's and Ricardo's hands. She turned to the small audience that had gathered. "And a thank you to all who assisted the police in catching our killer. It has been a difficult night, but we have come through it stronger. Despite the heartache that we are all feeling over the loss of our head chef and the arrest of one of our staff members, we rejoice that we have fought through this day. Tomorrow, we will rise," there was a groan at this, "and build an even stronger legacy."

It was a pretty, but vacuous, speech that gave the staff nothing to comfort them as they wept in their beds over how easily one of them had been killed, or how readily they had trusted Ross, a confessed killer.

"Well, that's all wrapped up," Kendra said with a tired smile. "Let's all get some rest before the final heaps of paperwork tomorrow."

"I have a few concerns," Isabel piped up at Rachel's side as soon as the crowd dispersed.

Rachel sighed and then drained her cup of lukewarm coffee.

"I'd like to go home and get some sleep. That's my only concern right now," Rachel snapped.

"Rachel, you know I wouldn't delay a case unless I thought it was absolutely necessary," Isabel insisted.

Her feisty friend groaned. She reached up to run her hands through her hair and Isabel noticed the slight tremor that resulted from an extreme overload of coffee in her system.

"Tell me you have evidence for a new killer and I'm all ears, but if it's just a hunch -"

"It's just a hunch," Isabel interrupted. "But a good one!"

"So, who is it?" Rachel asked, the doubt clear in her eyes.

"I don't know," Isabel admitted. "I just need to figure out a couple more clues."

"Okay, well, Ricardo and I need to carry on wrapping up the *solid* evidence we have on Ross. You have till tomorrow morning to figure out anything new," Rachel informed her tartly.

"Thank you," Isabel said gratefully. "Do me a favor and ask Ross where he got the bruises from on his neck. You might notice they're quite similar to Sarah's and would have rendered him useless in a fight. Have a long look at Ross and decide if you think he'd be able to take out a man like Fabian on his own."

"Tomorrow morning," Rachel called over her shoulder. "And I'll think about what you said."

"Alright," Colleen said, bustling up, "what do we do now?"

Her parents were looking to her for direction, which was an entirely new concept for Isabel. Isabel took a deep breath, collected her thoughts and forced her frazzled brain to work out a plan.

Chapter 10
A Final Kitchen Run

It had been strongly recommended, by an overly concerned Ricardo, that they first catch an hour or two of sleep before attempting to solve the murder case, but Isabel's mind was buzzing with too many questions to be quieted enough to sleep. One relatively obvious thing that Isabel could not put her finger on was the murder weapon itself. It was for this reason that she snuck back into the deadly quiet restaurant.

The dim grey light of early morning cracked through the dense darkness of the kitchen. Isabel navigated the cold tiles of the walls with her fingers until she found the light switch. It took a few seconds for the rows of fluorescent lights to thud and buzz to life, casting a sickly white glow over everything in the kitchen.

Isabel hastened to the chopping station she was most eager to inspect: Paul Salvador's. Just as she had seen earlier that night, the chef's knife was still missing from his pristine array of knives. It made little sense to her that anyone other than Paul would have been able to swipe one of his knives and bury it in the chest of Fabian.

"I thought I might find you snooping around here," Paul snarled at her. "You believe it's me, don't you?"

"Your knife was used to kill Fabian. Who else would've been able to steal it from under your nose?"

Paul advanced slowly on her, a menacing look played out in his piercing blue eyes. "Would you believe me if I told you my knife went missing a few days ago?"

Isabel raised a dubious eyebrow. "How convenient. What about the red stains on your chef's jacket?"

"That was from preparing your mother's meal. I dropped the spice lid in her broth, and it splashed out onto me," he explained. "I assure you it was not Fabian's blood, if that's where you're going with these ridiculous questions."

Isabel bit her lip. She was exhausting her clues rather quickly. "Would you like to tell me about your letters to Kendra?"

He scowled at her. "I requested Kendra remove Fabian and appoint me instead. What's wrong with that?"

"She refused you," Isabel pointed out. "It gives you motive to take matters into your own hands."

"Kendra refused me on paper," Paul explained with a tired sigh. "That was for the formal records. But we had a more private agreement between us. Fabian had caused far more trouble than he was worth, and his standard as a chef was definitely slipping. Kendra wanted him out as much as I did, and she was quite desperate for it to happen soon."

"And you were happy to stand by and wait patiently?" Isabel asked doubtfully.

"Yes," Paul replied, as though it was the most obvious answer he could give. "I built my career on my reputation. If it came out that I murdered a fellow chef to get to the top, my career and everything I've worked for, not to mention my entire life, would be over. I'd never be that stupid."

"But *someone* was that stupid and that desperate to get rid of Fabian!"

As the words tumbled out of Isabel's mouth, she realized who the most obvious killer was. Her jaw dropped open, and she gasped.

"You're not thinking…" Paul stared at her.

"Who else would benefit the most?" Isabel posed the question to him.

"But murder?" Paul shook his head and then froze. "She was the one that ordered my knives to go in for professional sharpening, and when they came back the chef's knife was missing."

"Perhaps she wanted to implicate you," Isabel reasoned, "and that's why she made sure your knife was used."

Paul paled again. "How did you find those letters from Kendra? On her laptop or -"

"No… I broke into your locker," Isabel explained.

"I never had those documents in my locker," Paul replied in a low voice, his dark eyebrows pinching in the middle. "There has to be an explanation. Let me see if I can talk to Kendra."

As Paul turned to leave, the lights flickered off, rendering them both temporarily blind. Isabel grabbed onto the ice-cold metal counter while she tried to gain her bearings. Slowly, her eyes adjusted to the dark-grey light of early morning as it trickled in through the upper vents.

She heard a man grunt, followed by a loud thump on the ground.

"Paul?" Isabel called into the surrounding space.

She could see a dark shadowy outline moving towards her and she ducked out of the way and down the second aisle of stovetops.

"Paul!" she shouted again as she hurried away from the terrifying shadow.

Isabel could feel the panic rising in her throat as she ran. Involuntary sobs escaped her throat, and she bit down on her lip to silence herself. Her foot hooked on what felt like an immovable rock and she plummeted to the hard, tiled floor.

"You just couldn't leave things alone, could you?" a woman's voice snatched at her through the darkness.

"I know it's you, Kendra," Isabel hissed into the darkness.

Isabel realized she had fallen over an unconscious Paul. He was lying face down on the ground and a touch of the dark, sticky substance next to his head told her he was bleeding heavily. The air smelled of the metallic zing of blood and disinfectant.

"He's not dead," Kendra sighed from somewhere in the kitchen. "Well, not yet. I'll finish the job later. I believe a vengeful Sarah Webber lost what little sense she has remaining and followed in her secret lover's footsteps by stabbing you and Paul in the same kitchen her tormenter Fabian worked. Yes," she paused, her voice closer than it had been before, "I believe that's got a nice ring to it."

Isabel scuttled away to a distant corner of the kitchen. Anger had replaced her fear. She could not stand the smug sound in Kendra's pompous voice, believing herself victorious for killing off her head chef, and getting someone else to take the fall for it. With a bitter taste in her mouth, Isabel recalled how Kendra had led her to suspect Paul, as well as Sarah and Ross, from the start. All a clever manipulation to throw Isabel off her own scent.

"I thought it was clever of you to steal one of Paul Salvador's knives. You must have been planning this for a while," Isabel stated boldly.

Kendra giggled from another side of the kitchen, her voice cold and empty. "If only you knew how much work went into implicating everyone but myself. It was interesting to watch you work. You played right into my hands."

"But you couldn't have known I'd be visiting your resort," Isabel frowned.

"No," Kendra growled, "my initial plan was to give your friend Rachel the free weekend, but she begged me to offer it to your low-class family instead. You can imagine my delight when I realized you enjoyed a good murder mystery as much as the next amateur sleuth."

"You used me," Isabel snapped at her, before leaping to a new hiding place. She knew Kendra was slowly tacking her through the positioning of her voice.

"And now I need to get rid of you," Kendra replied, her impatience coming to the fore.

"You incited Sarah to stand up to Fabian and attack him," Isabel said, realizing how cleverly Kendra had played all her employees. "You knew that Ross would go fight with him in Sarah's defense, thus putting other suspects' clues at the scene of the crime to mask your own presence."

"It was rather clever, wasn't it? There's practically nothing to tie me to the murder," Kendra laughed, her voice inches away.

Isabel heard the metallic click of a gun and dropped to the floor in an instant. The room exploded with light as the bullet fired, ricocheting off a pot a few feet above her head.

"That was a close one," Kendra snorted. "I almost got you, didn't I?"

"I have evidence that you planted documents in Paul's locker."

"Weak," Kendra said dismissively. "All those documents do is implicate Paul in the murder, and he won't be alive to defend himself. Of course, I'll have to plant this gun on him to explain the sudden appearance of bullets."

A second bullet blasted through the kitchen, shattering several glasses in the process.

"You made one mistake, though," Isabel informed her, her face cracking into a smile.

"And what's that?" Kendra asked with a sneer of annoyance.

"You confessed to me," Isabel explained simply.

Kendra's hollow laughter was so close, Isabel had to hold her breath for fear Kendra would hear her.

"Got you!" Kendra hissed as she rounded an aisle.

"Not so fast," Isabel said, wielding a frying pan. She caught Kendra on the head, causing the startled woman to drop her gun and grab onto a counter to steady herself.

"I don't go down without a fight," Kendra seethed at her.

Kendra reeled around and looked ready to go on the attack. There was another metallic click and Kendra's expression of confidence turned to one of shock when she felt her arm restrained behind her. A second cuff snapped around her other wrist and Kendra squirmed.

"Kendra Waters," Ricardo began loudly, "it is with great pleasure I would like to inform you of your rights."

"How did you know I was here?" Isabel asked in confusion. She flicked away the grateful tears.

Ricardo jerked his head in the direction of the entrance to the kitchen. Light flooded the room and Rachel, flanked by Isabel's parents, stood in the doorway.

"When your parents realized you were not sleeping in your bed, they knew you were out trying to solve the case on your own," Rachel explained.

"They also filled us in on all the clues you'd uncovered that proved Ross's innocence," Ricardo added with a proud smile.

"You were right about the bruising. He clearly had to walk away from his fight with Fabian if he wanted to stay alive," Rachel continued.

"But with Kendra, Fabian was not expecting a fight, so his guard was lowered, making it easier for her to get up close," Ricardo concluded. "We couldn't be sure until we heard Kendra confess herself. You saved this case, Isabel, and an innocent man from prison."

"And my parents saved me by getting you guys here," Isabel admitted. "I thought I was done for. Paul is somewhere here unconscious."

"I'm seeing to him," Colleen's voice shouted. "There's a lot of blood, but he'll be fine."

"Thank you," Isabel said with a smile. She swung her arms around her father's neck and squeezed him tightly. It was not long before she felt her mother's soft arms join the hug.

Chaper 11
A Second Chance

"This is delicious," Isabel approved with a dreamy smile. "Paul Salvador certainly has the title he deserves."

"I've decided I don't like Lobster Thermador after all," her mother concluded after pushing her polished plate containing a heap of lobster shell remnants.

"Well, you will most certainly tell our chef that you absolutely adored it," Robert informed her, "before we have another murder on our hands."

Isabel glanced over her father's shoulder and saw Ross sneaking a kiss onto a blushing Sarah's cheek. She smiled, grateful that everyone at the table, and she meant everyone, had had a hand in saving three people and putting one behind bars.

"Now, I have a question for you, laddie," Robert said as he slapped Ricardo on the back.

"Yes, sir?" Ricardo spluttered, nearly choking on a mouthful of food.

"When are you marrying our girl?"

Isabel choked on her own food and reached a hand for Ricardo's wine.

"I think you should come for a visit and inspect our little family home. I think the garden will do just perfectly for a wedding," Colleen added with a piggie snort.

"Well," Ricardo cleared his throat. "That all depends on if Isabel says yes."

Isabel felt her heart stop beating. She did not know whether or not Ricardo had actually proposed. Her fingers ached, and she realized she was squeezing his hand tighter and tighter.

"Well," Isabel managed in a strangled voice, "that all depends on when Ricardo actually asks me."

The End

Now that you have finished this cozy mystery, please consider posting a review on Amazon. It would be appreciated.

Printed in Great Britain
by Amazon